Charles Stuart Calverley, Walter Joseph Sendall

Literary Remains

With a memoir by Walter J. Sendall

Charles Stuart Calverley, Walter Joseph Sendall

Literary Remains
With a memoir by Walter J. Sendall

ISBN/EAN: 9783337093990

Printed in Europe, USA, Canada, Australia, Japan

Cover: Foto ©Andreas Hilbeck / pixelio.de

More available books at **www.hansebooks.com**

Yours ever
C. Halverley

THE

LITERARY REMAINS

OF

CHARLES STUART CALVERLEY.

WITH A MEMOIR BY

WALTER J. SENDALL.

WITH PORTRAIT AND ILLUSTRATIONS.

LONDON: GEORGE BELL & SONS,
YORK STREET, COVENT GARDEN.
CAMBRIDGE: DEIGHTON, BELL & CO.
1885.

PREFACE.

THE Editor's thanks and acknowledgments are due to the Rev. Dr. Butler, to Professor J. R. Seeley, and to Mr. Walter Besant, for the interesting contributions included under their respective names in the following pages.

Many others of Calverley's old friends and schoolfellows have also come forward with offers of assistance, in the shape of information and valuable suggestions; amongst whom should be specially mentioned Sir Robert Herbert, the Rev. H. N. Oxenham, the Rev. Charles Stanwell, Professor Lumby, and Mr. Austin Leigh.

LONDON, *May*, 1885.

CONTENTS.

MEMOIR.

POEMS.

TRANSLATIONS.

CONTENTS.

CHAPTER I.

SCHOOL AND COLLEGE.

SCARCELY had the grave closed over the head of Charles Stuart Calverley, when there began to be expressed, amongst those who had known him, a very general desire that some brief account of his character and career should be given to the world. It was thought, we may suppose, that the memory of one whose natural powers had made so extraordinary an impression upon his contemporaries, and whose published writings had given evidence of so very distinct and striking an individuality, should not be suffered to pass into oblivion, without some more enduring record than a paragraph in the newspapers, or an article in a magazine.

I.   B

It is in the belief that this was a well-grounded sentiment, and that those who have hitherto known "C. S. C." only as a writer of polished and epigrammatic verse, would be glad, now that he is gone, to learn something of the personality which lay behind those familiar letters, that the present task has been undertaken; and it may be permitted here to express a wish that the work, though truly in this case a labour of love, of delineating a character so unique, might have been committed into hands more practised than those of one, whom circumstances have long since consigned to the pursuit of avocations quite other than literary.

There are, indeed, in the uneventful record of Calverley's life, scanty materials for a full and lengthened biography; all that can be attempted is to place before the reader's mind some slight sketch of the man, as he appeared in the eyes of his familiar friends; employing for this purpose such personal reminiscences as those who knew him best may be able or willing to contribute.

A bright, sunny boyhood, fearless and careless; a youth full of brilliant promise, and studded with

intellectual triumphs; a manhood marked by no
stirring incidents, no ambitious struggles, no alter-
nations of failure and success—darkened, alas! in
later years, and brought to an untimely close by
the ravages of a fatal and insidious malady—such
are in brief the outlines of a career, which in itself
would seem to present little that is worthy of
record, and to possess but scanty claims upon the
attention of the general observer. But if the incidents and events of his life were thus trite even to
commonplace, yet his own bearing amongst them,
and the physical and intellectual personality which
marked each successive stage, would be found, if
accurately and adequately portrayed, to present a
striking and an interesting picture. From child-
hood upwards there never was a time when he failed
to impress in some enduring manner those amongst
whom he moved. His boyhood was distinguished
by feats of physical activity and daring, which
almost eclipsed even his marvellous precocity of
mind, and have already passed in school traditions,
like the deeds of ancient heroes, into the region of
myth and legend.

At a later period, though he was still remarkable for bodily strength and agility, it was the exceptional quality of his intellect which fascinated and enchained his associates. And as to this, there can be but one verdict amongst all who were even slightly acquainted with him. As an intellectual organism of the rarest and subtlest fibre, he stood altogether apart from amongst his contemporaries. And this not by virtue of any predominant excellence in one or other of the acknowledged lines in which men of talent or genius show themselves above their fellows. Brilliant and incisive in speech sparkling with epigrams, he was still neither a great talker nor a professed wit; capable of reasoning closely, he neither sought nor achieved reputation in debate; nor could he at any time have claimed precedence upon the score of acquired knowledge. Yet those who consorted with him derived from his conversation an impression which the most accomplished and encyclopædic of talkers might fail to produce. I do not know how better to express this phenomenon than by describing it as due to the spontaneous action of pure intellect. Without conscious effort, without the semblance of a desire for display, his mind appeared to *act* upon the matter in hand, like a solvent upon a substance. The effect of this was often as the revelation of an unknown force. A few words casually spoken became, as it were, a *fiat lux*, an act of creation. Let those who knew him at his best endeavour to account to themselves for the sense of power with which his conversation affected them, and they will, I think, be compelled to admit, that though his talk was often witty, always scholarly, and not seldom wise, yet what they marvelled at in him was neither the wit nor the wisdom nor the scholarship, but the exhibition of sheer native mind.

And herein, I think, to those who really knew him, will be found the all-sufficient explanation of that nameless excellence which all agree to discover in his writings, and which constitutes the key-stone of his reputation. About his most trifling, as about his most serious work, there is an inimitable and indescribable something, which is neither gracefulness only, nor is it merely fini s or polish or refinement, while at the same time it is each and all of these, and still defies analysis as securely as the scent and hue of a flower.

But whatever theory be accepted as true respecting the intellectual side of Calverley's character, this view of him alone will not sufficiently account for his personal ascendancy, nor for the unique place which he occupied in the estimation and in the affections of his friends. For he was fully as much and as deservedly loved as he was admired; and if he owed the one distinction to his natural gifts of reason unalloyed, he was indebted for the other, in no less degree, to that singleness and sincerity which were his most conspicuous characteristics upon the ethical side.

That he was absolutely free from all taint of littleness or doublemindedness, was manifest, it may be assumed, to the most careless observer; that he was an ardent lover of and seeker after truth for its own sake, that the windows of his soul were open to all the airs of heaven, and his heart waxen to the impress of whatsoever things are true, lovely, and of good report, was discernible by whosoever had eyes to see behind the very ill-fitting mask of seeming recklessness and indifference, with which it sometimes pleased him to disguise himself for the mystification of the overwise; but there was yet more in him than this, and to the few who penetrated into the inmost recesses of his nature, there was revealed a depth of tenderness, humility, and trust, the existence of which, even those who had a right to think they knew him well, might be pardoned if they never had suspected.

And it is doubtless here, in these central well-springs of his being, that the true secret of his influence is to be sought. Under whatever crust of indifference or reserve, behind whatever veil of inconsistencies, wilful or unintended—the beautiful real nature of the man shone or glimmered irrepressibly, winning all hearts by the power of sympathy and truth.

Endued, however, as he was, with infinite capacities of faith, in the matter of beliefs he was an incarnation of the principle of private judgment; and to mere dogmatic teaching, always and for ever impervious. " Unsanctified intellect," was, I believe, the term applied to him by a certain school at the University; unsophisticated intellect, would, I think, more fitly have expressed the fact, if it wanted to be expressed by an epithet.

An extraordinary carefulness and consideration for others was always a conspicuous characteristic in Calverley; and he endeared himself, particularly amongst his poorer friends and neighbours, by a hundred acts of unaffected kindness. In the Somersetshire village in which, previous to his marriage, his home life was chiefly spent, many stories are current, illustrating his active and sympathetic good-nature; and when the news of his untimely death passed like an electric shock through the circle of his acquaintance, nowhere was there awakened a feeling of sorrow more deep and true, than amongst the cottages of his old home.

Let it not be for a moment supposed that by these imperfect touches I am picturing to myself, or attempting to convey to the reader, the outlines of a faultless character. Calverley had important shortcomings, of which no one was more sensible than himself; and amongst these was an infirmity of will.   It is true that he was never subjected to the bracing stimulus of poverty, and that he was without those promptings of personal ambition which might have supplied its place; still some natural deficiency must be recognized here, and it must be confessed that, had he been endowed with a strength of purpose at all commensurate with his intellectual gifts, he would certainly have achieved work more truly worthy of his genius.

In his undergraduate days, though capable at times of the intensest application, he was somewhat prone to self-indulgence, and was a grievous sinner in the matter of lying late in bed.   During the months when he was (or ought to have been) reading for his degree, it was the daily task of one or two faithful friends to effect his dislodgment from his couch, before the precious morning hours should be wholly lost.   Upon these occasions, his chamber became the scene of a conflict, which reduced it to a condition resembling that of a ship's cabin at sea in a hurricane.   He, with his sturdy frame and resolute countenance, clinging, like "Barbary's nimble son"—

"By the teeth, or tail, or eyelid,"

to each successive covering, as one by one they
were ruthlessly torn from him, amid a storm of
good-humoured objurgation, charged with exple-
tives of every shape and size, ancient and modern,
of which he had a perfect arsenal on hand—so the
battle raged until, having conscientiously removed
every portable article of bed-clothing, his assailants
retired victorious, only to return in half an hour
and find him peacefully sleeping between the
mattresses.

"C. S. C." came of a good old English stock. He
was born at Martley, in Worcestershire, on the
22nd December, 1831 ; his father, then known as
the Rev. Henry Blayds, removing afterwards to the
Vicarage of South Stoke, near Bath.   The family,
who had borne the name of Blayds from the beginning of the century, in 1852 resumed their proper
name of Calverley, under which they had flourished
from before the Norman conquest in their native
county of York—having indeed a collateral connection with that Walter Calverley, the story of
whose ferocious deeds, and still more ferocious

punishment, is preserved in the pages of "A York-shire Tragedy," one of the many spurious plays attributed in an uncritical age to Shakespeare, and included in some of the earliest editions of his works. It was as Blayds that Charles Stuart won his reputation at Harrow and Oxford; at Cambridge he was known as Calverley.

Upon his mother's side, Calverley belonged to a branch of the ancient and honourable family of Meade; Thomas Meade, Esq., of Chatley, in Somer-setshire, having been his maternal grandfather; and to those who are interested in such speculations, a further examination of his ancestry, on both sides, would probably yield ample and satisfactory proofs of hereditary capacity.

Having passed through the hands of more than one private tutor, and after a brief sojourn (of no more than three months' duration) at Marlborough School, Calverley entered Harrow in the autumn of 1846, and from that time forward never ceased to be an object of interest and attention to a widening circle of friends and acquaintances. He is described as a curly-haired, bright-eyed boy, with a sunny

smile and a frank, open countenance; a general
favourite for his manliness and inexhaustible good-
nature, though already, it is said, distinguished for
a certain self-sufficing independence of character,
which remained with him through life, keeping him
always somewhat apart from his fellows, and in-
ducing him, even at this early age, to stand aloof
from the little cliques and coteries into which the
world of school divides itself as readily and naturally
as the world at large. He exhibited in an unique
degree, just that mixture of *insouciance*, reckless
daring, and brilliancy, which never fails to win the
unbounded applause and admiration of every genuine
schoolboy.

But it is only by an eye-witness that the story of
Calverley's school-days could be adequately told;
and I am fortunate in being able to lay before the
reader the following sketch by Dean Butler, the
late head-master of Harrow, his early companion
and life-long friend :—

"Charles Stuart Blayds was admitted at Harrow
by Dr. Vaughan on September 9th, 1846, being
then within four months of completing his fifteenth

year. He was placed in the Upper Shell, the highest Form in which a new boy could then be placed. He passed rapidly through the lower Forms, which were not then very numerous, and entered the Sixth Form in January, 1848. Here he remained till the end of July, 1850.

" It is difficult to give even a tolerably clear picture of a boyhood which was unlike any other that I saw as a boy, or have had occasion to observe since. He was unlike others in the absence of certain interests as well as in the brilliant gifts which were peculiarly his own. The Sixth Form of his time was not wanting in ability and vigour. Many of us were keenly interested in the politics and literature of the day. The year 1848, especially, was no ordinary year. I can remember the Head of our House one morning in February brandishing the ' Times ' over the bannisters, and announcing that Louis Philippe had fled from Paris in disguise. Then followed in dizzy succession revolutions, abdications, our own 10th of April, the Italian war, and the Hungarian revolt.

" Finally, at the end of the year, during the

Christmas holidays, the two first volumes of Macaulay's History were published, and received all over the country, even by young people, with a greediness of appetite still dear to the memory of men of fifty. Wordsworth was still living. Tennyson was on the point of mounting the Laureate's Throne. Ruskin was just startling the world with the first and second volumes of ' Modern Painters.' Dickens and Thackeray were in their prime. Further, the influence of Arnold's Life, lately published, was perhaps then at its height. This book and Keble's 'Christian Year,' so widely different and yet so accordant in much of their spirit, came home to the hearts of the more thoughtful boys.

" Once more, our Debating Society was a flourishing institution, though I own to remembering one debate on the ominous question whether it was worth while to continue it any longer !

" Now it must be confessed that in all the varied life, intellectual and religious, indicated by these books and events, Blayds had but little share. He had not a particle of cant or affectation in him, and he never pretended to be interested in either deep intellectual problems or high moral ideals which probably rather bored him.

" Though, as the sequel has proved, he possessed within himself a unique literary faculty which was destined in its way to approach perfection, he never, so far as I am aware, allowed it to peep out at school. His reading seemed hardly to extend beyond one or two favourites. A friend who saw much of him in those days confirms my own impression as to this. ' As for his literary tastes,' he writes, ' it always amazed me how much he seemed to know without reading, so to speak, at all. I should imagine that Virgil and Pickwick were, as you rather suggest, his favourite studies.'

" But though he took but little interest in the general intellectual life of the Sixth Form, he had one gift all his own, his power of brilliant Verse composition. He was a good Latin versifier when he first joined the School; and by the time he reached the Sixth Form, his work had attained a rare finish. In his very first term in the Form one of his exercises was thought worthy to be written out in ' the Book,' a distinction greatly

coveted, and hardly ever won so soon.   Another of
his earliest Sixth Form compositions seems worthy
of special notice,—a lively version, in the style of
Horace's ' Satires,' of the old fable of ' The Dog
and the Wolf.'   I do not think he ever wrote
again in this metre, but his version is full of *verve*
and lightness.[1]   It was, however, in September of
that year, when he was still three months under
seventeen, that he first showed what he could do in
Latin Verse.   His translation of part of Coleridge's
' Hymn to Mont Blanc ' is printed at the end of
this Memoir.   It may be safely said, that for
vigour, richness of rhythm, and sympathy with the
original, it will well bear comparison with any
verses written by a boy of his age.

"It is remarkable, therefore, that during his three
years in the Sixth Form he should only once, and
that in his last year, have won the regular prizes
for Hexameters and Alcaics.[2]   In the two previous

[1] The piece will be found below, see p. 119.
[2] The simplest explanation of this is likewise the most
probable, namely, idleness. Both at school and college,
Calverley needed to be spurred to exert himself. It is said
that one of the prizes which he did get, was only secured by

years both these prizes were won by F. Vaughan Hawkins, who was a year and a half younger than Blayds, and for two years beyond all comparison the finest scholar among his contemporary Harrovians, though he left the School a few days after his sixteenth birthday.

" In the ' Prolusiones ' of 1850, his prize Hexameters on ' Mare Mediterraneum ' end with a paraphrase of Byron's

" ' Roll on, thou deep and dark blue Ocean, roll ! '

which is full of feeling, and even eloquence.'

"The extreme ease and rapidity with which he hit off his verses may be illustrated by a story sent me by his devoted friend, the Rev. H. G. Southwell. I give it in Mr. Southwell's own words :—

" ' You are a better judge of the following verses than I am. I once asked Blayds to convert

" ' Raging beast and raging flood
Alike have spared their prey "

into Latin Elegiacs. We were walking towards

the determined intervention of friends, who locked him into his room until the needful exercise was written.—ED.

the School. He asked me some ridiculous question, which I forget now ; but just as I was leaving him, he said, 'I think this will do :—

> " ' Sospes uterque manet, talem quia lædere prædam
>   Nil furor æquoreus nil valet ira feræ.'

You will know whether they are sufficiently Ovidian to merit a notice. They were produced in about three minutes.'

" One story—not of his composition, but of his construing in school — may be worth recording here. The lesson was from the beginning of the Eighth Æneid. After a few minutes Blayds was 'called up,' and speedily warmed to his work. We soon awoke to the fact that he was doing it beautifully, using simple but choice English quite beyond our attainment. As he went on, there was a hush of admiring sympathy, which seemed to extend to the Head Master also. He was not pulled up till he had finished the whole of the lesson, probably some sixty or seventy lines.

" His appearance in those days was one of freshness and solidity. He always went by the name of 'Bull,' possibly from his having a short neck and a flat forehead. There was a thickset look about him, and an easy, casual manner, which was very attractive.

"One characteristic effusion may be mentioned, which has already found its way into print. We had just begun Russell's 'Modern Europe,' and the lesson for the day was the first Letter. During the few minutes of waiting in the lobby before school we had been laughing over some of the peculiarities of the style, but never dreamed that they were to be reproduced in the presence of the Master.

"The lesson began, and after a time Blayds was 'called up.' The question was casually put, 'How did the Gothic leaders conduct themselves in Italy?' The answer was at once given with pitiless accuracy, with due rhyming on 'bear' and 'parterre,' and with perfect appreciation of the central and the concluding cadences : 'They hunted the bear on the voluptuous parterre, the trim garden, and expensive pleasure-ground, where effeminacy was wont to saunter, or indolence to loll.'

"Though I was at the time, as indeed for nearly

three years, sitting next to the performer, and
though I have the liveliest recollection of his tone
and manner, strangely enough I cannot in the least
recall how the answer was received by the ques-
tioner. And yet much of the fun of the scene lies
in the fact that the Master and the Pupil were,
each in his own manner, two of the wittiest and
most humorous men of their time, unsurpassed
by any of their contemporaries in the keenest sense
both of the beauty and the absurdity of words.

"One friend who was sitting close to us, and who
had taken part in the previous chat in the lobby,
has a better memory than mine. His account is,
no doubt, correct. 'I *do* recollect Vaughan's re-
ception of "They hunted the bear." He suppressed,
but did not wholly conceal, his strong disposition
to burst out laughing, by resting his elbow on his
desk, and passing his right hand over his mouth.
Blayds had added to the effect of his recollection
of the passage by affecting to be a little uncertain
and hesitating about some of the words, sometimes looking down, and then looking straight at
Vaughan.'

" One of Blayds' most remarkable gifts was his verbal memory. Probably it largely accounted for his exquisite ear, and his power to reproduce, with a grace perhaps unequalled, the metres—I do not say of Virgil and Horace, here he has been more than rivalled—but of Tennyson, Browning, and most of the poets and versifiers of our day.

" One story illustrative of his memory, and perhaps of his boyish character, is given me on the authority of Mr. Southwell :—

" ' A master, whom we will call X,[1] went into his room one night after the orthodox hour for putting lights out, and found Blayds' candle burning. X, in his unemotional way, ordered Blayds to learn the First Book of the Iliad, and say it in a week's time. Immediately after X's exit from the room Blayds relit his candle, and either learnt, or, I must think, refreshed his memory by reading what he already knew, the aforesaid First Book. At any rate, after lessons were over at *first* school on the following morning, Blayds presented him-

[1] " X " was the late Mr. Harris, for whom Calverley entertained the most affectionate regard.—ED.

self to X, and expressed his wish to say his task.
It is recorded that a slight trace of wonder passed
over X's countenance ; but he took the book, and
bade Blayds go on. Tried in divers places throughout the book, he was found to have committed it
all to memory, and his fault was expiated.'

"If Mr. X ever learned the secret of this rapid
tour de force, he had quite enough shrewdness and
humour to enjoy it.

"Another of Blayds' gifts was that of sketching
in pen-and-ink. His caricatures were inimitable.
One, which long remained in my school copy of
the 'De Oratore,' and is, I hope, surviving somewhere under mountains of Harrow papers, represented Hannibal having just reached the top of the
Alps. The great general was perched on one
sharp peak of the Mont Cenis, 'chucking' a
javelin into the air, and skipping like a boy let
out of school ; while on a neighbouring peak might
be seen the upper moiety of a panting, flustered
elephant, with trunk erect, retaining just enough
presence of mind to ejaculate 'Hooroar!'

"No account of Blayds' Harrow days would be

even tolerably complete which left out of sight his athletic reputation. He was not, indeed, a distinguished player at cricket, or football, or racquets, though he took an active part in all these games, but his daring leaps were the wonder of the School. It may be doubted whether, even at the time, some of them did not, in Thucydidean phrase, ' win their way to the fabulous.'

" One, I remember, was connected with a certain high white gate which we had to go through in our jumping parties to the Kenton brook. Blayds was said to have ' gone at ' this gate in cold blood, and to have carried away some of the spikes from the top !

" Another of his jumps, which caused great amusement at the time, cannot be appreciated without a lively recollection of the locality. The ' Grand Plateau ' of the School Yard stands some eight feet ab ve the historic ' milling-ground,' being separated from it by a wall of about four feet high. One day, while waiting for the 4 o'clock Bill, Blayds casually went at the wall with his hands in his pockets, just touched the top with his foot, and alighted on his head, twelve feet below. All anxiety for his fate was soon set to rest by his reappearing in the yard, and again going at the wall, only this time with a little less *insouciance*. The result was an easy victory.

" But his *chef-d'œuvre* in audacious jumping, and that by which his name will be chiefly remembered, is his clearing the stone steps of the Old School building—a space of fully twenty-one feet, if measured obliquely from top to bottom, the lowest step, however, being about nine feet below the highest. There was then one step less than at present, and the paving of the yard was not, as now, asphalte, but gravel. In the presence of the School Custos and a group of admiring comrades, Blayds took a run from the door of the 'Governors' Room,' and reached the bottom in safety, only just touching the last step with one of his heels.

"This part of our subject may be not inappropriately illustrated by two stories of Oxford and Cambridge days. They come to me from my old Harrow friend, Alfred Blomfield, now Bishop of Colchester, and from H. G. Southwell.

"'In Christ Church meadows,' writes the Bishop, 'there was a broad ditch, now, I think, covered, or concealed by a wall: and on the bank of this ditch grew a willow whose branches formed a Y or fork some three feet above the ground, just wide enough for a man's body to pass through. Blayds would leap *over* the ditch and *through* the fork: a feat requiring both strength and precision, and involving serious damage in case of failure. I will not be absolutely certain that I myself saw him do this, though my recollection is that I did; but I am quite certain that it was done, and I remember the spot well.'

" Mr. Southwell's story is even more surprising.

"'At Cambridge,' he says, 'I remember an instance of his activity and indifference to danger. He was walking with me in Green Street; a horse in a cart was drawn up on to the pavement, the horse being on the pavement, the cart in the street. With his cap and gown on, and his hands in his pockets, and with a very short run he cleared the, I should say, astonished steed, and alighted smiling on the other side.'

" No one can feel more than I the superficial and therefore unsatisfactory nature of the above sketch. It contains no grave touches. It may be the fault of the writer that he cannot with truth, or at least with veracity, insert any. I had a warm affection for my dear friend all through our Harrow days, and we were constantly together; but somehow grave topics did not seem to come natural to him, and we instinctively avoided them. He was always good-humoured, genial, full of fun, with something of the 'Bohemian' in him, only tempered intellectually by an exquisite and severe appreciation of classical form and rhythm, and socially by great kindness of disposition and a very affectionate heart. With the graver interests of School life he did not appear to sympathize : his own life was blameless, he got into no troubles, but he was never regarded as one of the governing forces of the School.

" He was a sweet-tempered and most amusing companion, with a prompt, terse, and finished wit seldom found in boys. To think of him as he was in those happy school days is to think of what is keen and bright and sunny. It was reserved for the noontide of his life to reveal fully the treasures of delightful humour and satire that lay within him. I speak only of what came to view in its charming but unpretentious dawn."

The following reminiscences by another of his earliest friends [1] may fitly close the records of his School life.

" Just after he left Harrow he had a great escape, from his habit of chancing what he jumped at. He was staying at the King's Head, and went out before breakfast on to the lawn at the top of the garden. At the bottom was a hedge of some height, high enough to conceal what there might be beyond, except that it was clear there was a drop. This was quite enough for him ; he rushed at the jump, cleared the hedge, and found himself dropping into a well on the other side. With a strong effort he managed to throw himself forward, and get a clutch at the top of the well with his hands, and with great difficulty draw himself out.

" The same absence of fear that he showed in this way, he also showed in all his transactions with the

[1] S. Austen Leigh.

masters. When a monitor, he was playing at
stump-and-ball in his tutor's yard, and hit a ball to
leg, over the road, through the drawing-room window of a master who lived there. His companions
were rather frightened at what had happened ; but,
without a moment's hesitation, just as he was (not
by any means a presentable object), he bounded on
to the wall, and down the drop, into the road, and
rang the front-door bell of the master's house.
The said master had been startled by the appearance of the ball through his window, and answered
the door himself. Blayds quietly asked for his ball.
The master began to complain of his window being
broken, and also at the state of Blayds' dress and
appearance. Blayds only remarked that he was
sorry he had broken his window, but that he had
happened to make an uncommonly good leg hit, and
he wished to have his ball back ; and he got it.

" I remember one instance of his great powers of
versification. He came into my room one Tuesday
afternoon to ask me to go out jumping with him.
I told him I could not go because I had a set of
Greek Iambics that must be done that day. He

said, ' Nonsense, that won't take you long.' My answer was that it certainly would, for at present I had not arrived at understanding the English— some lines of Shakespeare. He took up a pen and paper, sat himself down, and bade me read out the English. I did so, and as I read, slowly, it is true, but with hardly any stop, he wrote them down in Greek Iambics, good enough at all events quite to pass muster.

"He was always a most delightful companion, never out of temper, and I need hardly say entertaining in the extreme, and though somewhat apt to disregard school laws himself, I never remember his having in any way attempted to make me do the same. The last time I saw him was a good many years ago at the Reading Station. We had not met for years, and I only hope he was half as glad to see me as I was to see him. At all events he did not forget to make himself pleasant. My train was due in fifteen minutes; he proposed a walk, and so entertaining was he, that I gladly missed my train, though at the cost of some inconvenience."

Calverley's career at Oxford, though a failure

for academic purposes, was distinguished by a series of *tours de force*, intellectual and physical, sufficient to have furnished forth a dozen ordinary reputations. He won the Balliol scholarship by a marvellous copy of Latin verses, written off with such rapidity as to be almost an improvisation. His exploits in the way of daring and impossible jumps were long talked of and pointed out, and their memory may perhaps still linger amongst the traditions of the place. Having, in common with the other students, to prepare a Latin theme, to be submitted on a given day at a *vivâ voce* lecture, Calverley appeared in the lecture-room provided like the rest with a neat manuscript book, the pages of which were entirely blank. He had trusted to luck, and hoped that he might escape being "put on." Luck failed him, and in due course the examiner called upon " Mr. Blayds." Whereupon he stood up and, to the amazement of those who knew the real state of the case, proceeded without the least hesitation, and in calm, fluent tones, to read from his book the exercise which he had not written, and of which not a word had up to that moment been composed.

Among the academic functions established at
Balliol, and possibly also at other Oxford colleges,
was a ceremony known as " Collections," for which
Cambridge experience furnishes no equivalent.   It
appears to have consisted in a kind of intellectual
and moral stock-taking, at which the assembled
students were put through an examination upon a
variety of subjects, sacred and profane, receiving
praise or reprobation in accordance with their
deserts.   The following episode occurred during
one of Calverley's appearances at " Collections,"
the Master (Dr. Jenkyns) officiating.   *Question :*
" And with what feelings, Mr. Blayds, ought we
to regard the decalogue ? "   History relates that
Calverley, who had no very clear idea of what was
meant by the decalogue—his studies not having
lain much in that direction—but who had a due
sense of the importance both of the occasion and of
the question, made the following reply : " Master,
with feelings of devotion, mingled with awe ! "
" Quite right, young man, a very proper answer,"
exclaimed the master.

It must indeed have been felt that a youth im-
bued with these just and admirable sentiments

would guide his words with discretion, and might even be trusted never to "speak disrespectfully of the Equator."

The good opinion which he thus obtained by subtlety did not, however, avail him long, and during his second year of residence his connection with Balliol and with Oxford was brought to an abrupt termination. His biographer, while chronicling this fact, must at the same time not fail to insist that the offences against discipline for which he justly suffered, were due to an exuberance of animal spirits rather than to any graver form of delinquency. That at this period of his career he vexed the souls of dons, and maintained a perpetual warfare with constituted authority, is to be admitted and regretted. Into most of his escapades, however, there entered an element of humour, which, while it does not redeem them from censure, invests them with an interest in relation to his special cast of mind. Calverley's coolness, wariness, and consummate dexterity of speech, rendered him at all times a dangerous opponent in an encounter of wits; he had, moreover, when provoked, a knack of employing words, in themselves most artless and innocent, in such a way as to affect the other side with an uncomfortable sensation of being quizzed.

Of the numerous stories current respecting his Oxford days, some of which went the round of the newspapers at the time of his death, it will be sufficient to notice one or two, the authenticity of which can be vouched for.

The following incident is related rather on account of the punning verses to which it gave rise, than for its own intrinsic interest. The election to scholarships at Balliol took place upon St. Catharine's Day (November 25), and on the evening of the same day the newly-elected scholars received formal admission, in the college chapel, at the hands of the Master and Fellows. When Calverley's turn came to be presented to the Master for the purpose of taking the customary oath upon admission to the privileges of a scholar, the fact that he had quite recently been indulging in a pipe forced itself upon the attention of Dr Jenkyns, who had the strongest dislike to tobacco,

I.   D

On withdrawing from the chapel, the Master turned to the Fellows who accompanied him, and said, " Why, the young man is *redolent of the weed*, even now ! "   It was no doubt this remark of the famous old Master of Balliol, which afterwards suggested to their unknown author the following lines, which, like the " Sic vos non vobis" of Virgil, received their first publication in the form of a mural inscription :—

> " O freshman, running fast to seed,
>   O scholar, redolent of weed,
>   This motto in thy meerschaum put,
>   The sharpest *Blades* will soonest cut."

To which Calverley at once replied :—

> " Your wit is tolerable, but
>   The case you understand ill ;
>   The Dons would like their *Blayds* to cut,
>   But cannot find a handle."

Dr. Jenkyns was the most conspicuous figure in the University of his day, and there was something in his somewhat pompous (though in truth most kindly) nature, which invariably struck sparks when brought into collision with this audacious and keen-witted undergraduate.

The keeping of dogs in college was, it is needless to say, strictly prohibited at Balliol, and was especially reprobated by the Master; it is almost equally needless to add that the prohibition was systematically evaded; and one of the most incorrigible offenders in this respect was Calverley. Meeting him one day on the way to his rooms, with a tawny nondescript treasure trotting at his heels, the Master exclaimed, "What! another dog, Mr. Blayds!" "Master," was the wily response, "they do tell me that some people think it is a squirrel." This reply, while it committed the speaker to nothing, was really calculated to mystify the Master—not, it may be guessed, himself a very close observer of specific distinctions—for the creature in question, though undoubtedly a dog, did to an inattentive eye bear no slight external resemblance to the other-named animal.

He advanced at Oxford the reputation he had brought with him from Harrow, of being one of the best writers of Latin verse of his time; the Hexameters, with which he obtained the Chancellor's prize in 1851,[1] still remain one of the most beautiful of his many beautiful compositions.

It is customary for these prize poems to be printed and published, with the author's name and that of his college attached. When Calverley's manuscript was sent to the press, it bore, in anticipation of his impending doom, the following signature :—

CAROLUS STUART BLAYDS,

e COLL BALLIOL.

prope ejectus.

It was actually so printed, and it was only through the opportune interference of one of the college tutors that it was not so given to the world. When called upon for an explanation, Calverley is said to have declared that "those tiresome printers would do *anything*."

Calverley quitted Oxford in the beginning of 1852, and in the following October was admitted as a freshman at Christ's College, Cambridge. It was here that the present writer first became acquainted with him. He was then at the zenith of his powers,

---

[1] Subject, *Parthenonis ruinæ*.

mental and bodily. Short of stature, with a powerful head of the Greek type, covered thickly with
crisp, curling masses of dark brown hair, and
closely set upon a frame whose supple joints and
well-built proportions betokened both speed and
endurance—he presented a picture of health,
strength, and activity. In disposition he was un-
selfish, and generous to a fault; without a trace of
vanity or self-esteem; somewhat reserved amongst
strangers, though bearing himself at all times with
a charming simplicity and frankness of demeanour;
slow to form friendships, but most loyal and constant to them when formed; a faithful, affectionate,
whole-hearted, thoroughly loveable human soul;
with an intellect as keen, swift, and subtle as any
that ever tenanted a human body.

It is not at all easy, indeed, it is hardly possible,
to convey by description an adequate idea of the
singular charm of his conversation. It must always
be understood that though he said many good
things, he was by no means an inventor and utterer
of *bons mots*. Instead of expending itself in a
succession of flashes, his wit was, as it were, a

luminous glow, pervading and informing his entire
speech, investing the thing spoken of with a novel
and peculiar interest, and not seldom placing it in a
vivid light, at once wholly unexpected and wholly
appropriate. There was also in him a great quick-
ness both of sympathy and of apprehension, enabling
him to seize upon your point of view with rapidity
and precision; and when to this is added a perfect
honesty of intellect, free from any warpings of
prejudice, egotism, or other pregnant source of
self-mystification, the result is a set of conditions
for rational intercourse of a rare and very special
kind, the pervading feature of which is a whole-
some atmosphere of security, an almost physical
sense of comfort and *bien-être*—like the feeling of
warmth and good cheer—which those who have
experienced it will acknowledge to be as attractive
as it is uncommon.

Cambridge discipline is, or is said to be, of a
more liberal and less coercive character than that
which obtains at the sister University, and Calverley, who moreover had gathered wisdom from
experience, fell readily enough into the ways of

conformity and obedience to rules. Though not, perhaps, exactly a favourite with the older and severer type of Don, who never quite knew how to take him, he was cordially appreciated by the authorities of his own college, themselves mostly men of a younger generation than the academic petrifactions of an earlier school. At no time, indeed, during the whole of his Cambridge course, did Calverley evince the slightest inclination to embroil himself with the ruling powers; and it is altogether a mistake to suppose that, careless as he may have been of conventionalities, he had in his nature anything of the real Bohemian. Nor was he, either then or at any other period, a mere unprofitable idler; and if not what is usually termed a reading man—that, namely, and nothing else— he was emphatically a man of reading; a genuine lover of literature, and with a considerable knowledge of books.

Composition in Latin and Greek was his favourite intellectual exercise, or, it might rather be said, recreation; the famous " Carmen Sæculare," the translation of Milton's " Lycidas " into Latin hexameters, a beautiful version of " John Anderson " in Greek Anacreontics, and several other of his most successful efforts, dating from this period. At this time, too, he was developing that incomparable vein of humour, that inimitable compound of serious irony and pure fun, blended with subtle and delicate banter, by which afterwards, in "Verses and Translations," and still more decisively in " Fly-leaves," he " took the town by storm," and affected the reading world with the enjoyment of a new sensation. The Byronian stanzas in which he celebrates the praises and the works of Allsopp and of Bass, were in manuscript before he had taken his degree ; and it is curiously characteristic of his many-sided genius to note that at the very time when, with keen appreciative insight, he was penetrating the secret of Milton's majestic verse, and was reproducing those mournful, tender, or triumphant strains, in diction not less stately, and in numbers not less harmonious than the master's own—he could also let his sportive fancy play in airy raillery around the same pathetic theme, depicting, in a few telling strokes of mirthful mockery—

"How Lycidas was dead, and how concerned
  The Nymphs were when they saw his lifeless clay,
And how rock told to rock the dreadful story
  That poor young Lycidas was gone to glory."

Amongst his humorous compositions of this date, the " Pickwick Examination Paper " has obtained a notoriety which entitles it to a passing mention.

Probably no one amongst the Cambridge men of that day (excepting, perhaps, the late James Lempriere Hammond) equalled Calverley in close and comprehensive familiarity with the writings of Dickens. The notion (conceived at first as a pure joke) of making a great living author the subject of a competitive examination, would suggest itself naturally enough to one who had all his life been winning prizes for proficiency in the lore of ancient bards and sages, some of whom, perchance, held a far lower place in his affections than did the creator of the immortal Weller. The ingenious syllabus of questions which has attracted so much attention, is not, however, interesting only as a measure of Calverley's curiously minute acquaintance with the masterpiece of Dickens; it deserves also to be noticed on account of the winners of the two prizes which were offered to the successful candidates. The first prize in the competition, which was open to all members of Christ's College, was taken by Mr. Walter Besant, the second by Mr. (now Professor) Skeat.

Calverley's appetite for humour, and his faculty of extracting it even from the most unpromising material, are oddly illustrated by the following "Notes," taken after he became a fellow of his college, and accidentally preserved amongst his papers:—

Notes taken at College Meetings.
At Meeting, February 28th, 11½—2.

Remarked by the Master.—That no people give you so much trouble, if you try to extract money from them, as solicitors.

By the Jun. Dean.—Except, perhaps, parsons.

By the Senior Dean.—The latter possibly because they have not got the money.

By Mr. A.—That a ton weight is a great deal of books.

By Mr. B.—That it is just one o'clock.

By Mr. C.—That that is likely, and that in an hour it will be just two.

This record of the proceedings of a learned

deliberative body is worthy of a place beside Mr. Punch's "Essence of Parliament."

To the above specimen of Calverley's humour may be added the following *jeu d'esprit* which appeared in the columns of the "Pall Mall Gazette" in 1865, when middle class examinations were in their infancy : [1]—

"Berries from the Tree of Knowledge.

"'By all means let classics be retained : *as the handmaids of more useful branches of study.* Valueless themselves, they may be made a vehicle to convey what is invaluable.' Thoroughly satisfied of the truth of this principle, an Oxford M.A. of eminence—he took (he mentions) high botanical honours, though 'comparatively weak' in Latin and Greek—determined to test it at a recent middle-class examination. The result was a paper in Latin prose translation, of which, he admits, the candidates 'could make nothing,' but which he still

[1] For this quotation I am indebted to a notice of Calverley which was published in the same journal a few days after his death—"Pall Mall Gazette," 29 February, 1884.

'cannot but consider a move in the right direction.'
We subjoin it; adding also the interpretation, as
sent—which, we may add, the words seem to us to
bear, ' vix aut ne vix quidem " in some places—for
the benefit of the mere classic.

" Translate :

" ' Morum te nigram juraveris : morum vero al-
bam fecisti. Solvi, vixdum rubum cæsium, vaccinium
tuum myrtillum : teste virgine berberin circumvoli-
tante, et baccâ sambuci patre tuo.   Dederas et
cheirographum : sed atramentum oxycoccus palus-
tris.   Equidem non pendo unius fragarii ribes taxi
baccæ simile: permittam tamen omnibus chiococcum,
te rubum Idæum prorsus exstitisse : vaccinium
autem, senior, dic.'

" ' You may swear yourself black, Berry; but you
have made a mull, Berry.   I paid your bill, Berry,
as soon as due, Berry; as the young woman in the
bar, Berry, and your father, the elder Berry, know.
I don't care a straw, Berry, for a goose, Berry, like
you, Berry; but I'll let folks know, Berry, that
you've made yourself a regular ass, Berry ; and
whort'll Berry senior say ? '

" The style of the Latin is more or less that of Cicero's letters; though we think we would certainly have expressed some of the ideas—towards the end especially—in different language. We are not altogether satisfied of the rectitude of the ' move.' Surely it is pushing the Oxford theory a little too far. We commend the English version (fragments of which seem, unaccountably, familiar to us) as a useful *memoria technica* to the notice of mothers and governesses."

No account of Calverley's undergraduate life at Cambridge would be complete without some allusion to his musical talents. He had a remarkable ear, and possessed a voice of great purity and sweetness. The musical gatherings which from time to time took place in his rooms, are amongst the pleasantest of the many pleasant memories which cluster round those cheerful and hospitable quarters. When in the mood, he would take his seat at the piano and rattle off a series of extravaganzas, made up for the nonce out of the popular airs and operas of the day, interspersed not unfre-

quently with songs of his own composing ; he also
possessed the rare accomplishment of being able to
whistle a perfect accompaniment to the instrument.

A general election which took place during
Calverley's residence, and was the occasion of a
memorable outbreak amongst the younger members
of the University, deserves mention, although he himself took no active part in it, on account of a stirring
episode, of which his college became the scene, and
which has never, so far as the present writer is
aware, been chronicled in prose or verse.   It
would require the pen of a Thackeray and the
pencil of a Leech—*plena leporis Hirudo*—to do
justice to it, and it happened on this wise.

The contest for the representation of the University was keenly watched and debated in undergraduate circles, by reason chiefly of the extraordinary popularity enjoyed by the Liberal candidate,
Mr. (now Mr. Justice) Denman.   So great was the
excitement, and so noisy were the demonstrations
with which, in those days of open voting, the sup-
porters of either party were greeted from the
thronging galleries, that the Vice Chancellor (Dr.

Whewell) deemed it prudent to order the exclusion of all undergraduates from the Senate House during the hours of polling. This invasion of their ancient privileges was indignantly and violently resented by the youthful champions of Liberalism. A bonfire was made of the hustings in front of the schools. The intrepid and despotic Vice Chancellor was himself threatened, and had to be escorted to his residence in Trinity by a strong bodyguard composed of Masters of Arts. On the morning following these events a decree was issued, directing that in every college the gates should be closed at an early hour, all persons *in statu pupillari* being required to keep themselves within. The effect of this sweeping and somewhat ill-advised measure was, that when the appointed hour arrived almost the entire undergraduate population was found to be in the streets. Forming themselves into a compact body, four or five abreast, they marched from college to college, demanding that the gates should be thrown open. In not a few instances the demand, through the undisguised sympathy of the garrison with the cause of the

besiegers, was at once complied with. Service
was proceeding within the college chapel when the
wave of rebellion reached the massive oaken gates
of Christ's, and thundered for admission. The
sudden appearance of the college porter, pale and
trembling, apprised the congregation, consisting of
the fellows and a few scholars, of what was taking
place. The Master stopped the service, and, putting himself at the head of his forces, marched in
an imposing procession of some ten or twelve sur-
pliced figures to the scene of action. Arrived at
the inner side of the barred and bolted gate, the
Master, having obtained a brief silence, proceeded
to remonstrate with the insurgents, desiring, in tones
of authority, to be informed whether they knew
" who he was ! " This display of vigour elicited
a storm of uncomplimentary replies, for, to speak
truth, the late Dr. Cartmell, though in every way a
most admirable Master of his college, was not so
generally popular in the University as he no doubt
deserved to be. Meanwhile, an unexpected diver-
sion was being effected by the enemy. Flanking
one side of the college buildings was Christ's Lane,

a private road belonging to the Society, into which is a side door opening from the college kitchens. Once in the year this road is closed to the public by means of a strong oaken bar, which at other times is hinged back and padlocked to a post. Whilst the main body were parleying at the gates, a strong force, guided by members of the college, hastened round to the lane, unshipped the bar, and employed it as a battering-ram against the kitchen door. News of this second attack was speedily conveyed to the Master. Taken thus in the rear, Dr. Cartmell wheeled gallantly round, passed rapidly across the quadrangle, and, traversing the kitchens between grinning rows of scouts and cooks, arrived at the precise moment when, its panels battered in, the door flew violently open, the victorious mob rushed by, bearing back Master, fellows, scholars, and cooks in one undistinguishable mass, swept irresistibly through the court, and, overwhelming the bewildered porter, opened the gates, and vanished from the citadel almost before its discomfited defenders had time to realize what had happened.

I. E

This incident brought hostilities to a close.
Owing chiefly to the good sense and forbearance
of the several college authorities, the ebullition
everywhere subsided as quickly as it had arisen;
the door in Christ's Lane was rebuilt more strongly,
and the University resumed the even tenor of its
way.

Of these great events Calverley, as has already
been said, was a spectator only; a sufficient proof,
if proof were needed, that the freaks of insubordi-
nation of the Oxford days indicated a purely
transitory and evanescent aspect of his character.
Meanwhile his list of University honours was not
unworthy of his reputation and abilities. He gained
the Craven Scholarship, which is the blue ribbon of
undergraduate distinctions, in his second year; the
Camden medal for Latin hexameters fell to him
twice, the Greek Ode (Browne's medals) once, and
he also took the Members' Prize for Latin prose.
He finally came out second in the first class of the
Classical Tripos of 1856, and within two years
afterwards was elected fellow of his college.

He continued for a year or two after this to reside

at Cambridge, taking private pupils and sharing in
the work of the college; and in 1862 he made his
first appearance in public with *Verses and Translations.* Three years afterwards he was admitted to
the bar as a member of the Inner Temple, and
joined the Northern Circuit; having in the meantime vacated his fellowship by his marriage with
his first cousin, Ellen Calverley, of Oulton, in York-
shire. He now took up his abode permanently in
London, and applied himself to the work of his profession, attending circuit regularly until his active
career was interrupted by an accident which, though
little was thought of it at the time, was destined to
have far-reaching consequences.

Of this period of Calverley's life the writer of
these pages, being then and for some years afterwards resident abroad, can give no account drawn
from personal recollections. There is reason to
believe that, brief as was the duration of his active
connection with the bar, it was long enough to
create an impression highly favourable to his prospects of future distinction. As sometimes happens
with men endued with a powerful imagination, he

found the study of law in itself sufficiently attractive
to render comparatively easy the acquisition of legal
knowledge, which his wit, resourcefulness, and acute
reasoning faculty would have enabled him to turn
to good account, had time and opportunity offered.
But this was not to be.

The accident of which mention has just been
made, occurred in the winter of 1866-7, about a
year and a half after his call to the bar. Calverley
was skating at Oulton Hall, near Leeds (the residence of his father-in-law), when he tripped and
was pitched heavily on his head, inflicting a severe
blow over the right eye. Although the injury was
sufficiently serious to need surgical treatment, no
other attention was paid to it, and no permanent
mischief was perceived or anticipated. When, however, he was induced, by symptoms which some
time afterwards supervened, to consult an eminent
London physician, he was declared to have sus-
tained a concussion of the brain, the effects of
which, though they might have been alleviated, and
possibly altogether counteracted, by a short period

of absolute rest taken at the time of the accident, were then such as to render it necessary for him to forego the strain of body and mind inseparable from the work of his profession.

From this time it may be said that for all the active business of life Calverley was practically laid upon the shelf. He had indeed still before him many years of tranquil happiness and enjoyment, in the society of wife, children, and friends, nor was he debarred from the pursuit of his favourite studies; still he chafed under the restriction from active work laid upon him by his physical condition, and, as has already been hinted, he was without the all-mastering strength of will through which a sterner or a more ambitious nature, if gifted with equal intellectual endowments, might have found in a forced period of leisure and retirement the path to solid and enduring fame. Thus it has happened that, although the work which he has left behind him is indeed exquisite of its kind, it is, as to much of it, unpurposed and fragmentary; reaching no-where to the full height of his genius, and leaving

almost wholly unevidenced his deeper qualities of
mind and heart.

Engraved in facsimile from a pen-and-ink drawing.

CHAPTER II

RECOLLECTIONS.

TO some of the readers of James Payn's charming volume of "Literary Recollections," not the least attractive of the many delightful pictures which it contains will be found in a brief notice of Calverley, dating from a long vacation passed at Grasmere, in company with the present writer, in the summer of 1857. Calverley had already graduated, and was making holiday during those well-remembered months; I myself, then in my third year, was engaged in acquiring that modicum of mathematics which the University in those days exacted, as the price of a degree, from all aspirants to classical honours. We two occupied a small cottage [1] (often revisited since) upon the

---

[1] Now expanded into Baldry's shop and lodgings, kept still by the same kind and friendly hosts, whose first tenants we were.

road leading from the Red Lion down to the lake. Payn, who was just entering upon the career which he has since pursued with such brilliant success, had taken house with his young wife and two (I think it was then two) bright toddling bairns, about the centre of the village.

My 'coach,' Wolstenholme,[1] then a fellow of Christ's, was staying with a reading party at Ambleside. We were all good walkers (not excluding Payn, who, I think, does something less than justice to his own prowess in this respect), and in the course of the summer had rambled over every mountain and valley in the district. The ascent of Scawfell was achieved from Wastwater by Wolstenholme, Payn, Calverley, and myself. We took Great Gable on our way, descending thence upon the Sty Head; and by the time we reached the mile or so of rocky boulders leading directly to the summit of Scawfell, had certainly taxed our staying powers somewhat severely. It was here that Payn lagged a little behind, and, on rejoining us, was

[1] Now Professor of Mathematics at the Indian Civil Engineering College, Cooper's Hill.

greeted by Calverley with the ready jest, duly recorded in the "Recollections," "The labour we delight in *physics* Payn." The aspect of the Lake District has changed considerably since those days. The railway, which now encircles it from Keswick to Windermere, had then no point of contact nearer than Kendal. A single coach ran daily along the road which is now traversed during the season by a never-ending procession of crowded vehicles. The number of those to whom our British Alps are familiar ground has multiplied a hundred-fold, but the friendly intercourse which subsisted between the natives and their visitors of thirty years back, can hardly be extended to the swarming holiday-seekers of to-day. With this change of manners much of the charm which year by year drew thither a small but faithful band of pilgrims, has vanished. But at the time of which I speak, the old simplicity still prevailed; at feasts and wrestling-matches, in farm-homesteads, and the parlours of old-fashioned, unpretentious inns, the visitor was everywhere welcomed as a friend; and Calverley, whose easy bearing and frank good-humour made him a general favourite, loved to brace his faculties and freshen his sensations by contact with the kindly and strong-natured dalesfolk.

For one who enjoyed life keenly, and who possessed both means and leisure, it is somewhat surprising that Calverley should have travelled so little abroad. Two journeys to Switzerland and one to Norway comprise, I believe, the sum total of his achievements in this direction. The first of these tours, which took place before he quitted Cambridge, was performed in company with a few college intimates, one of whom was Mr. Walter Besant, whose regard for his departed friend has prompted him to furnish me with the following reminiscences of college days, with notes of the foreign journey which he and Calverley undertook together.

"Christ's College, which Calverley entered, has of late years occupied a position somewhat different from many of the so-called small Colleges—it is itself larger than any College at Oxford except one or two—in the good luck it has always enjoyed with its men. No other College, for instance, has, for its size, a nobler roll of 'worthies.' Of these Milton,

Darwin, Leland, Paley, and Bishops Porteous and
Kaye, are, perhaps, the best known. The entrance
of Calverley coincided with the commencement of a
long period, during which the College greatly distinguished itself, year after year, in the Honour Lists,
especially in the Classical Tripos. Among the men
who were undergraduates there in Calverley's time,
or soon afterwards, was, first, his own contemporary, John Robert Seeley, now Regius Professor of
History, and the author of ' Ecce Homo.' In addition may be mentioned Ebden, now Chief Clerk of
the Colonial Office ; John Peile, Senior Classic in
1860, and afterwards Tutor of Christ's ; you yourself, now governing West Indian Islands ; Hales,
now Professor of English Literature at King's Coll.
London ; Skeat, now Anglo-Saxon Professor at Cambridge ; Hensley, now Senior Physician at Bartholo-
mew's ; Robert Liveing, now in the first rank of phy-
sicians ; the present Bishop of Toronto ; Lee, translator of Virgil and Horace ; Wren, who stands at the
gate of the Indian Civil Service ; George Henslow,
Botanist, and many others who have shown intellectual activity and made honourable mark in the

world. Among the Dons were Gunson, the Tutor; Gell, now Bishop of Madras; Archdeacon Cheetham, then Lecturer in Classics; and Wolstenholme, now Professor at Cooper's Hill.

"There is no doubt in my own mind that the taste or fashion for reading which certainly existed among the undergraduates at Christ's at this period, was largely due to the example of Calverley and Seeley. They were both men who stimulated their contemporaries and juniors, but in different ways— Calverley, perhaps, because he represented learning and scholarship in its most graceful and attractive form, aided by a delightful wit and genius of the rarest kind—and Seeley because he was in daily life and character such an exemplar to his contemporaries as the continual exercise of high and noble thought and pure aims can make a young man. It was a rare chance indeed for one College to possess these two men at the same time.

" The daily life of the men five-and-twenty years ago, was considerably different from that which has been, I am informed, more recently adopted. The way of life was simpler, and in some ways much rougher.

The dinner was served at four, which surely is the most detestable hour ever invented. It was generally a very bad dinner, and consisted wholly of joints, not over well roasted, with potatoes and small beer. Other things were to be had if you called for them, but they were put down in the bills. Every College then brewed its own ale. The Christ's brewer gave us strong ale or "College," Bitter, and Small. No one in those days pretended that he could only drink claret—indeed there was very little claret in the College at all, and there was no wine put on the table.

" After Hall the men divided into little sets and went in turn to each other's rooms and drank port and sherry till six. I dare say it was not good for the boys to be drinking fiery port, but it generally only amounted to one bottle between four or five men, and if it was wrong it was pleasant. I hear that now they drink little but Apollinaris, which may be right, but cannot from any point of view be considered pleasant. At six o'clock there was Chapel, in those days much more of an institution than at present. After Chapel the reading men generally

shut themselves up till ten or so with tea and books,
and at ten there were other gatherings with pipes
and beer till midnight. Every afternoon all the year
round the boats went down the river—in those days
Christ's had two in the first division and one in
the second. This carried off some seven-and-twenty
men; of the remaining fifty perhaps half walked
down the river on the banks to see the boats, and
the others went to play racquets or fives, or to walk
to Madingley or Grantchester. Two or three out
of the whole perhaps wasted their afternoons in
billiard-rooms. In summer of course there was
cricket. Calverley's favourite game was racquets,
which he played extremely well; he also played
fives, and he rode a good deal, but he never, I believe, went on the river. Once a week, on Saturday,
there was a Whist Club, at which he was sometimes
present, though he never played. It seems wonderful, after all these years, to relate, that at midnight, when the whist was knocked off, we always
sat down to a great supper with copious beer, and
after supper to milk punch and talked till four! And
yet some of us survive! On Sunday morning, when

chapel was at half-past nine, there was always a break-fast after chapel in someone's rooms—a good honest breakfast, with cold pie and beer and the 'Saturday Review,' then a young and astonishingly lively paper —and after breakfast a long walk till Hall time. A healthy life it was, with plenty of talk, plenty of feasting, plenty of play, and for many of us plenty of reading, besides the necessary work for the abomi-nable Senate House. There was also plenty of enthu-siasm. Perhaps you may remember one man who could recite the whole of Tennyson's 'In Memoriam.' There was reading aloud, and we had gods. First and foremost, we worshipped Carlyle. I worship him still, although he has now been proved to have had a temper—as if that matters! Maurice, whose memory I love, though I have forgotten so much of what he wanted to teach, was the second god ; and Kingsley—why does nobody now ever write such a beautiful story as 'Westward Ho!'—was third favourite. But with him must be placed Dickens and Tennyson. There were one or two who had tried Browning, but his day was not yet come. Other gods we had, but these were the chief, and among us moved Calverley, always finding out every man who was clever, or amusing or interesting, and always with something new, something that had pleased him, and must therefore please everybody —and Seeley, always grave and serious, yet naturally and without affectation, and because the problems of the world were already upon him.

"It was in the year 1860 that our walking tour in the Tyrol took place. My recollections of the expedition, now more than twenty-four years ago, are by this time rather hazy. For instance, I do not remember exactly how long it lasted, nor could I follow our route on the map, nor have I any journal or record, except a little note-book full of rough sketches which I made on the way. Among these there survived until quite lately a little pencil sketch by Calverley himself, but I have now lost it, to my great regret.

"The party consisted of Calverley, Peile (since Tutor of Christ's), Walton of St. John's, and myself. Walton, who unfortunately died of consumption seven or eight years later, was then a Fellow of St. John's, Fifth Wrangler in his year, and

was then, or immediately afterwards became, one of
Llewelyn Davies's curates at Marylebone. He was
a hard-working clergyman, and I have often gone
with him on his rounds about his parish, and seen
certain strangely-furnished upper and lower chambers in the wilds of Marylebone. He gave me, in
fact, my first introduction to the London poor—I
suppose those chambers have long since poisoned
all the poor I saw—and I never tired of admiring
the way in which he continually ministered to them,
always cheerful,though always engaged in the clergyman's constant endeavour to divide half-a-crown
exactly and equally among thirteen deserving cases.
However, he left the cares of his poor behind him
when he took that holiday, and was as entirely happy
as if everybody in the world was rich and contented,
and as if Marylebone existed not even in imagination: at all events, everybody in the party, to
which the world was for the time narrowed, was
young, and we were all going to get rich some day:
and we were quite persuaded, whatever our own
personal ambitions might be, that Calverley, for his
part, had only to name the particular pinnacle on

which he proposed to stand for the admiration of the world, and that it would be at once set aside and reserved for him like a stall at the theatre. I do not think it does any harm for young men to believe greatly in one a year or two older than themselves, and very much cleverer. The year was one of those when it rains without ceasing. Somebody announced, for instance, when the rain had gone on without stopping until the middle of July, that there would be no summer that year, because the Zodiac was taken up for repairs. They took it up again, you remember, in the year 1879.

" I joined Walton at Heidelberg, where he was staying, and we got on by easy stages, and stopping at a great number of places, as far as Innsbrück, where we were joined by Calverley and Peile. The verses in 'Verses and Translations,' on a Rhine steamboat tour, commemorate the first part of the journey, when he was with Peile. I have often felt defrauded because nothing of the later wanderings found its way into the same little volume.

" We started on our walk from Innsbrück, and

I left the other three men some five or six weeks later at Meran. Where we wandered in the interval I know not, but we wandered a good deal, knapsack on back and staff in hand. Sometimes we slept in huts on the mountain-side, and breakfasted off bad coffee and a dish of fried eggs; sometimes there were not enough beds to go round, and we had to toss up for those that were available; sometimes we got wet through, and as we carried no change, we had to robe ourselves with blankets. Everywhere there was magnificent scenery, with pine forests and mountain streams; every day there was climbing, more or less; every night one was dog-tired. I have vague recollections of the Zillerthal, for example, and of a place called Linz or Lienz; and of a strange place beside a lake, where there was a great hotel, and a steep hill beside it, up which Walton made us all climb before dinner. But these recollections are vague. One or two memories, however, stand out with greater clearness. The first is of a certain evening in the Zillerthal after dinner; the now well-known singers came in, a party of half-a-dozen peasants,

and sat down and sang to us, accompanied by the
zither, the sweet Tyrolese songs which have since
become so popular ; but in these days they were
only known to a few ; the Tyrol was comparatively
unexplored, and I think none of us had ever heard
the songs before, or even so much as seen a zither.
I distinctly remember Calverley's face ; you know
how, when he was really pleased and interested,
his expression became grave, and his features set,
as if he was rapt and absorbed in the thing which
then engaged him. I have never seen him so
entirely pleased and interested as on that evening.
Presently, when the singers had finished, he broke
out in short ejaculations, railing upon the stupidity
of English people who do not teach their peasants
how to play or sing. Then, because Walton had the
sweetest and most musical voice possible, and Calverley, as you know, could take his part, we tried
two or three simple English part-songs, in which Calverley sang second and Walton bass. I forget what
they were—'Spring's Delights,' 'Care, thou canker
of our joys,' 'Oh! who will o'er the downs,' and so
forth—simple ditties all. After that, Walton sang

them a song, and Calverley followed with one, which was at that time a great favourite with him. You yourself wrote the words, to an air which he found somewhere or other. They began, ' Fare thee well, where thou art lying.' I remember the first verse only, but I have never forgotten the air, which is singularly sweet.[1] I have taught it to a good many, since, but I have never met anyone yet who knew it, or where it came from. The people were greatly

[1] Respecting the air of which Besant here speaks, the following will be read with interest. It was in the May Term of 1856 that a young man, with an accent and manner slightly foreign, was paying a visit to the University, and was frequently in Christ's College, where he had friends. He had a wonderful gift of sketching, which he freely exercised for our amusement, and he played and sang with a facility of execution less common then than it has since become amongst educated Englishmen. This young man's name was George Du Maurier. Among his favourite songs was the well-known one of Byron's, beginning "There be none of Beauty's daughters." This he sang, without notes, to a simple and pathetic air, with which none of his hearers were acquainted. The air took Calverley's fancy, who played it afterwards from memory, and the score was written down from his playing. Some verses, slight enough in themselves, but intended to give expression to the peculiar pathos of the music, were, as Besant says, composed for the occasion, and were adopted by

pleased, not so much at the singing—it was a small
thing compared with their own, though Walton's
voice was not one that you can hear every day—but
at the strange thing that any young Englishman

Calverley, whose singing of them will be remembered by
many, and as they have not appeared in print they may be
quoted here.   They were as follows :—

> " Fare thee well !   Where thou art lying ;
>   The clouds for ever weep,
>   And the breezes whisper. sighing
>   In a soft dirge and a deep.
>   And the skies, that wont to love thee,
>   Are a folded shroud above thee ;
>   And the flowers, that blossom o'er thee,
>   Are bending to adore thee,
>   And all things fair deplore thee,
>   Where thou art laid to sleep !

> " But thy pure and gentle spirit,
>   That could no longer stay,
>   Doth a holy place inherit,
>   In a land far, far, away.
>   'Neath the cypress, dark and lonely,
>   Lies thy body buried only ;
>   Thou hast found a home for ever—
>   There, where death no more shall sever,
>   And the golden light fades never
>   In the bright eternal day."—W. J. S.

should know how to sing. It was contrary to their experience; they thought that Englishmen only paid and listened.

"Another day I remember. We slept in a shepherd's hut high on the mountains; having got there in the evening after a long climb up a steep hill, from some place which I forget. There was not much for dinner, I know, but there was something : in the morning we rose at daybreak, still stiff and tired, and found that the only thing for breakfast was a dish of eggs, fried in a tin, and some had coffee—nothing else, not even bread. We started, therefore, for the day's work in that condition in which, according to the moralist, one ought to rise from dinner, namely, hungry. The proposed work was going to be very simple, only to cross over what was described to be a low Pass; we thought we should probably manage it with great ease by ten o'clock or so, and get a solid breakfast then. Illusory hopes ! We started about five, and we began by losing our way, which wasted three hours or so; then we struck the right path, as we thought, and began again. For forty days and forty nights, or thereabouts—

it seemed more to me—we toiled up the steep face
of the mountain over turf. Whenever I go up a
mountain, I always experience exactly the same
sequence of emotions. First there comes a deadly
fatigue in the legs, which presently goes away of
its own accord, leaving a sort of limb-sulkiness;
then follows a nightmare in which I am firmly persuaded that I have from the beginning of all things
been everlastingly going up a hill, everything else
having been a dream, and that there will never be
any cessation or rest from going up a hill for the
future *in sæcula sæculorum*. In the midst of this
nightmare I become conscious, and it adds an intensity to the present suffering, that the whole
misery was voluntary: I need not have gone up this
hill. It was by my own deliberate choice. Why
did one choose? What madness drove one up this
mountain? I am quite certain that other people
have exactly the same sensations, and hate climbing
as much as I do, but they are too proud to say so.
Presently, on this mountain, one became aware that
the turf was covered with little drifts of snow; then
that the turf was disappearing altogether, and then

that the snow covered everything, and that it was getting deeper. One would have liked, at this point, to sit down and go to sleep, but you cannot sit in snow up to your neck; besides, Calverley and the other men were stalking a-head with such disgusting freshness and vigour. I do not know how long the 'work,' as Alpine men very feelingly call it, lasted, but we trudged on, mounting higher and higher, and the snow getting continually deeper, and it must have been long past mid-day when we stood upon the summit of our 'low' Pass. We found afterwards, on looking at the map, that we had come the wrong way, and had climbed quite needlessly over a Pass estimated at ten thousand feet, instead of six thousand. I thought at the time, and I still think, that the true altitude must have been at least sixty thousand. I remember the scene as we stood on the ridge and gazed around, perfectly well. Calverley, who looked as if he had not turned a hair, stood, resting his hand on his alpenstock; Walton, a little breathed, stood beside him; Peile, jealous for the honour of a Westmoreland mountaineer, refused to confess himself tired; and the fourth man, alas! too far gone for pretence, unreservedly sitting on his knapsack. Around us the peaks rose, one behind the other, the summer sun upon the snow, a miracle of wonder and of beauty. Everybody, however, confessed to being hungry, and there was nothing to eat. We had with us a small flask filled with Kirschen schnapps, about half a pint, which went round once or twice. A spoonful of schnapps is not a bad thing on the top of a low Pass. This despatched, we began to descend. Some way down—I feel that I am not speaking scientifically—we came upon a glacier, whether a piece of a big glacier or a little one, I know not; it was dangerous, I suppose, but the going was comparatively easy, except when one had to jump a crevasse. These were fortunately narrow, but they had a cold and steely look which made one feel as if they were much broader. Presently we passed across the ice and got into snow again, and after that we came upon the turf, and then the mountain stream with its rapids and its cascades, and then the pine forests, and so down, down, down, while the sun sank lower, and at last we hit upon a road, and presently, long after the sun had gone down, and after walking in the shadows of the evening along the dark rough track amid the pine woods, we came to an inn where at nine o'clock we got the most heavenly meal ever served, though it consisted of nothing but veal cutlets. Fifteen hours without food made even the Tyrolese bread delicious. I was not and am not ashamed to own that I was thoroughly and completely knocked up. But Calverley did his last half-mile with as elastic a tread as his first, and as cheerful a countenance as he had shown at the beginning. One of the things which made him the most delightful companion in the world, was that his temper never gave way, not even under little irritations of the moment, which too often make weaker brethren use 'language.' He was never put out by any of the accidents of travel, by bad food, or by insufficient food, or by fatigue, or by losing the way, or by bad beds, or by anything. Possibly an ill-tempered member of the party might have disturbed his serenity, but I doubt it.

"A third day.

"This time I remember the name of the place.
It was called Heiligen Blut, and there was a village
church, with a bone-house at the back of it full of
skulls and thigh-bones, once belonging to the rude
forefathers of the hamlet. It was from this place
that we were going to make our grand ascent of the
Gross Glockner, the great achievement for which
we had come all the way from England, an ascent
which was not made after all. The Gross Glockner
is a very big mountain, so big and so steep, that it
is creditable to have climbed it. I had, for my
own part, thoughts and ambitions concerning the
Alpine Club, to be attempted after the performance
of this feat. We had talked a great deal about it.
Two of us certainly had never done any Alpine
work before this, and in fact never seen the Alps
until that year, so that we were anxious to try the
perils of which we had read, the cutting of steps in
the ice, the cautious steps one after the other tied
together by a rope, and the passing of one night
at least upon a ledge. There is always a ledge, and
generally a man who walks in his sleep, but does
not tumble over, though his friends are kept awake

by their anxiety on his account. Well, I have never experienced these perils, and never slept on a ledge, and now I suppose I never shall. Certainly, when we really arrived at the foot of that mountain, and had our first talk with the guides, and learned what we should have to do, and how long it would take, one of us began to feel very doubtful whether the glory was worth the fatigue, and whether mountains, as a rule, do not look better from their lower slopes. But we did not attempt to go up that mountain. The summer had been very wet, and the guides decided, after talking the thing over, that they would not venture to take us. So that was settled for us, and I daresay the other men were disappointed—in fact, I am quite sure they were—and the only other survivor besides myself, will doubtless, if he remembers the thing at all, remember that I was not disappointed. As for the mountain itself, it was veiled in cloud during the time of our stay at Heiligen Blut. We had, however, one good view of the Peak : it was during dinner, and after a long day of rain. A German staying at the inn suddenly jumped up, left the table—moved, I take it, with the prophetic instinct —and rushed into the open air, where we saw him, to our great astonishment, solemnly raising his hat, and bowing to the ground, as one that boweth low to King or Kaiser, shouting, ‘Er ist rein! Der Gross Glockner ist rein!’ So it was, and a splendid peak it looked, with the sunshine upon it, standing out against the sky, steep and icy and inaccessible, and as one that sayeth, ‘You try to climb up my sides? You?’ Then we made the acquaintance of the parish priest of Heiligen Blut, and a very good fellow he turned out. How we began to know him and to talk with him I do not remember, but he dined with us one evening, and the next evening he invited us to his own house. We smoked pipes, drank light wine, sang songs, and had a miscellaneous entertainment. Somebody found a zither, and some of the village girls and men came to sing, and we made a night of it, and ended with clasping hands all round and crying with enthusiasm, ‘Nieder mit Napoleon! England and Deutschland!’ —at least some of us did. Well: we were very young. The next day was Friday and *jour maigre.*

His Reverence appeared, but he gave us the coldest of greetings and was absorbed in his Hours, which, like the hours of the clock, lasted all the day.

"I believe this is the sum of my memories of this summer holiday. I have had a great many holidays since then, *outre mer*, and in many other lands, but none quite so full of brightness and happiness. It goes without saying that Calverley was always the life and soul of the party; that he was always full of wit, pleasantness, and cheerfulness; and that, whatever he did, or whatever he said, or in whatever company he found himself, he carried always his own fine taste and the grace and charm of manner which was peculiarly his own."

CHAPTER III.

CALVERLEY AS A WRITER.

WHAT will be Calverley's permanent position in literature, is a question which must be settled by the critics. The present writer has no pretensions to determine it, and must decline to attempt the task. Satisfied as those who knew him may be, that the full depth and extent of his powers are very imperfectly manifested in his writings, it is nevertheless by these that he will be chiefly judged; and this at least is certain, that the world will never consent to form an estimate of his merits more lowly than was his own, who was at all times as little prone to see any excellence in himself, as he was prompt and eager upon all occasions to recognize it in others.

Assuming that all competent judges are agreed as to the superlative goodness of his classical compositions and translations, I will only observe in this place, that in all such work his professed aim and object were faithfully to represent, not the sense merely of his author, but also the form and expression. It is not sufficient, in his view, that the thoughts and ideas of the original should be reproduced, in language of itself however appropriate and idiomatic, by the copy; this is indeed indispensable, but this is not enough; there must, in addition to a wholly faithful *sense*-rendering, be also to some extent a *word*-rendering, and even if possible a *form*-rendering. Wherever this path is ventured upon by an unskilful or incompetent workman, it is apt to lead him down a perilous incline of merely verbal resemblance, into a bathos of doggerel and sheer nonsense; just as, on the other hand, a given version may correctly enough represent the bare meaning of the original, and yet be in itself a mere tasteless paraphrase, of the Tate and Brady order of merit. There is also this danger—of which I am reminded by a friend and former pupil of Calverley's, himself an acute scholar and an admirable translator—that in working upon

I. G

the method indicated above, the ingenuity of the
operator may be made too apparent, and the work
show too plainly the mark of the tool. Still, I
think, one sees that Calverley's method is in itself
the right one ; it certainly increases, almost indefi-
nitely, the translator's difficulties ; and proportion-
ately enhances the merit of success.

It must be understood that in speaking of *form-
rendering* as one of the objects aimed at in Calverley's translations, I am as far as possible from re-
ferring to any kind of metrical imitation. Calverley
totally disbelieved in all attempts to force modern
language (or at all events modern English) into the
mould of a classical metre ; and even where this
appears to have been successfully accomplished, he
denied that the result was to reproduce the rhythm
(i.e., in the truest sense, the *form*) of ancient
poetry. His views upon this subject are expressed
at some length and with characteristic humour, in a
paper which he contributed to the " London Student " (October, 1868). The whole article, which
will be found in the Second Part of this volume, is
extremely interesting, as an example of critical

analysis; and a perusal of it will, I think, be sufficient to satisfy the reader that in Calverley's opinion the business of a translator of classical poetry is to preserve as much as possible of the rhythm of his author's verses, and that this cannot be achieved by any endeavour, however successfully carried out, to imitate their scansion.[1]

Calverley's own measure of success in translating upon his own method is, I venture to think, almost if not quite unrivalled, and constitutes the distinctive mark of his performances in this department. The better to illustrate my meaning, I will cite two short specimens of his translation, one from Latin into English, and one from English into Latin. A very few lines will suffice, and our first example shall be the following stanza from an ode of Horace :—

---

[1] Upon the contents of this paper the late Professor Conington wrote to Calverley as follows :—

"I read with great delight your paper on English Hexameters and Alcaics in the 'London Student,' agreeing thoroughly with what was said, and enjoying greatly the manner of saying it."

" Audivere, Lyce, di mea vota, di
    Audivere, Lyce. Fis anus, et tamen
        Vis formosa videri,
        Ludisque et bibis impudens ; &c."

which Calverley thus translates :—

" Lyce, the gods have listened to my prayer :
    The gods have listened, Lyce. Thou art grey,
        And still wouldst thou seem fair ;
        Still unshamed drink, and play, &c."

Upon this translation it is to be observed, in the
first place, that it is pitched in the precise key of
the original—neither higher, nor lower, nor other ;
and that besides adhering closely to the meaning of
the Latin, it also indicates with fidelity the swing
and rhythm, not merely of the particular metre,
but of the particular passage ; reproducing with
wonderful exactness a certain effect of intensity and
compressed denunciatory force—partly the result
of a skilful arrangement of words—which is not
more apparent in Horace's Latin than in Calverley's English. There is indeed in the latter
nothing at all of the endeavour (ambitiously aimed
at by some translators), conjecturally to represent
the manner or the phrase in which Horace, had he

been an Englishman writing in English, might
have been expected to satirize the modern "Lyce;"
but it is a conscientious and supremely intelligent
attempt to recast in English both the sense and the
form of Horace's Latin words.

For our other example, we will select a single
couplet from the " Lycidas :"—

> " For we were nursed upon the self-same hill,
>   Fed the same flock by fountain, shade, and rill."

There is before the world more than one Latin
version of these lines, by scholars of acknowledged
reputation ; that of Calverley's is as follows :—

> " Uno namque jugo duo nutribamur, eosdem
>   Pavit uterque greges ad fontem et rivulum et umbram."

Without claiming for the latter any special
superiority upon the ground of its perfect fidelity
to the meaning, I would venture to assert that no
other version that can be quoted, approaches it in
the exquisite precision with which it follows the
cadence and movement of Milton's stately measures.

The truth is that for work of this kind Calverley
was magnificently equipped, both by nature and
(so to speak) by art. He was saturated with

Virgil before he had left school; he had a most
retentive memory, an inexhaustible command of
language, and a faultless ear ; and holding kinship,
as he did, with all forms of genius, his imagination
readily took fire at its touch, and burned with a
corresponding flame.

The qualifications needed in a translator who
should follow the high and uncompromising standard of excellence by which Calverley worked,
would seem, at first sight, to be somewhat incon-
sistent with those of a successful parodist, who may
be regarded as a kind of pseudo-translator, in so
far as what he aims at is a deliberately partial and
one-sided representation of his original ; and if, as
common consent appears already to have decided,
Calverley is to be reckoned the first of English
parodists, the reason spontaneously suggested by
the view taken of him in this notice would be, that
his natural powers were greater than those of any
other modern writer who has cultivated this peculiar talent.

And accordingly we find, I think, that the
element which chiefly distinguishes his work of

this class is the element of mastery and strength. " Lovers, and a Reflection," inimitable and unutterable nonsense though it be, is an extremely powerful piece of writing; while of " The Cock and the Bull" I venture to say that it will stand for all time, a monument of vigorous, effective, and most justifiable satire.

The first-named of these two celebrated burlesques is, indeed, little else beside pure fun. It is too absurd to be satire, too ridiculous even to be ridicule. If it is to be taken in the light of an admonition, it is truly a loving correction, so empty of censure, and so replete with kindly mirth, that the accomplished authoress herself, who is its object, may (and, indeed, does) enjoy it and laugh at it as heartily as all the rest of the world. What moved Calverley to the perpetration of it I do not know, but it was probably written without much premeditation. He has been reading (we may conjecture) a well-known and deservedly popular volume of poems; his sense of humour is tickled by certain seeming incoherencies of thought and expression, observable in the first poem of the

series, called " Divided ;" he "spots" here and
there, with the eye of experience, sharpened by
long practice on his own account, a too palpable
sacrifice of sense to the exigencies of sound ; and
while he is musing upon these things, a gentle
afflatus steals upon him, and the thing is done; he
thoughtfully takes up his pen, and in a moment—

" In moss-prankt dells which the sunbeams flatter,"

and all the rest of the inspired nonsense, is rattled
off without an outward symptom of emotion
stronger than a pensive chuckle.

It is pleasant to be able to record that the
cordial intercourse already subsisting between
poetess and poet was in no way disturbed by the
appearance of " Lovers, and a Reflection ;" and
that, to the last, the brilliant scholar and man
of letters possessed a valued and appreciative friend
in this variously gifted lady, with the creations of
whose graceful and womanly fancy such liberties
had been taken by his audacious muse.

Of Calverley's parodies of Browning and the so-
called mystical school, a somewhat different account
must, I think, be given. He here strikes in ear-

nest, and with a purpose.   The present writer,
who is himself a humble and sincere, though often a
sorely puzzled, admirer of Browning, feeling at the
first a little scandalized by the uncompromising
directness of Calverley's attack upon " The Ring
and the Book," once ventured to suggest remon-
strance, and, with a view of convincing him of the
error of his way, repeated to him those noble lines,
beginning—" O lyric Love, half angel and half
bird "—which form the conclusion to the opening
chapter of the story.   Calverley said little, but his
face flushed, and his eye lit up, and it was easy to
see that no want of appreciation of the strength
and beauty of Browning's verse had prompted his
assault upon those mannerisms and obscurities of
style, which he looked upon as a grave literary
offence.   His own clearness and, so to speak,
point-blank directness of mental vision, rendered
him especially impatient of all the crooked and
nebulous antics and vagaries of thought or speech
in which writers of the modern transcendental
school are pleased to indulge; and his parodies of
this class must be regarded as a genuine and out-

spoken expression of resentment that so much genius should seem to take so much pains to be unintelligible. I am aware that to speak of this school of writers otherwise than in terms of respectful panegyric, will savour of profanity in the eyes of those amongst their admirers who are not so much critics as votaries. To such it may not be amiss to suggest, that in matters of literary taste, as well as in graver matters, *securus judicat terrarum orbis;* and that if the common sense of mankind had not long ago delivered judgment upon the affectations and extravagances of style against which Calverley's satire is directed, the word mannerism would either not have been invented, or would have acquired a different connotation.

See " Verses and Translations," p.17.

CHAPTER IV.

THE END.

IN the second part of this volume will be found all that remains of interest from Calverley's pen, not included in the works already published under his name.

Specimens of his really remarkable talent for drawing will also be found in the frontispiece, and here and there in other places. His readiness with the pencil was well known to his friends, whom he occasionally delighted with sketches, humorous or otherwise, in which he displayed a fertility of invention and a delicacy of execution such as would have done credit to a professed artist. A few of these have been reproduced in a manner to convey some idea of the originals, though failing to do full justice to the laborious minuteness of detail which was a characteristic of his work in this kind.

These desultory gleanings will, it is hoped, be received with a welcome by his admirers, and, if they do not add much to his reputation, will, at least, be considered to be not unworthy of it. I have little more to add to this imperfect and fragmentary sketch. To the world, the whole interest of Calverley's life consists in what he was rather than in what he achieved; or, to put it otherwise, his writings are chiefly valuable as the expression and visible token of an unique personality. And of the more conspicuous features of his mind and character, his candour, his tolerance, and his inimitable humour, the writings which he has left us are indeed the best and most adequate exponent. The more serious side of his nature, unsuspected, perhaps, by the majority of readers of his delightful verse, was nevertheless familiar enough to those who knew him, at all events, in his later years. "He was as light-hearted and fond of mirth," writes one,[1] "as any man who ever lived, but I never heard one word from him that was either

---

[1] Letter from Professor T. R. Lumby.

irreverent, profane, or ribald, or calculated to wound the feelings of anybody. He cut his jokes (and oh, how clever they were!), but they were not at the expense of anybody or anything." "Those who had the happiness of knowing him personally," says another, " would need no literary proof that C. S. C. was far indeed from being the ' idle trifler of a passing day.' Of sacred subjects he spoke habitually with deep and unaffected reverence, as one who recognized the essential limitations of human faculties, and was content to wait in faith for the clearer vision behind the veil." [1] One who had visited him, during Cambridge days, at his house in Somersetshire, says : " I mention this visit, the memory of which is full of pleasure, because of the impression it left upon me of one particular kind. It was this—that there never was a man more thoroughly, more truly domestic in his tastes and habits, and more likely by disposition and habits to make a home bright. . . . Years passed of which I could say little. But in

[1] Letter from the Rev. H. N. Oxenham.

1870 I visited him in London. Days instead of years might have been the intervening time. It was plain enough that in his married life, as before in his old home, the very simplest domestic pleasures were what he cared for most, but some of the conversation we had at this time was grave enough. I urged him, as doubtless other friends had done, to set about some work that would engross him and give his powers full play; and I found that to be unable to find the kind of work or the special subject was a matter of real regret to him."[1] To these sketches by intimate friends may be added, in conclusion, the following picture, for which I am indebted to Professor J. R. Seeley :—

" I made Calverley's acquaintance at Cambridge in the Michaelmas Term of 1852, when we both became members of Christ's College. We were of the same year as undergraduates ; nevertheless we did not take the degree at the same time, and those who consult the Cambridge Calendar will not find our names in the same Tripos list. Calverley followed the ordinary course and took his degree in

[1] Letter from the Rev. Charles Stanwell.

1856 ; I took mine in 1857, availing myself of a privilege which belongs—or did belong—to those who have entered at a bye-term. Both Calverley and I remained in the College for some time after graduating. He got his fellowship, if I remember right, in 1858 ; I got mine in 1859. We held college lectureships and took private pupils; in fact, followed the ordinary routine of those times.

"In 1861 I went to London, where I remained till 1869. I fancy Calverley stayed a little longer in Christ's; but if so, no long time passed before he too was living in London, married and called to the Bar. Thus we were again within reach of each other, and remained so for something like eight years. Since 1869, when I returned to the University, we only met by accident, but in 1875 we found ourselves for some weeks neighbours at Grasmere. Again we took walks together and talked over old times. Then, too, I made acquaintance with his boys. The eldest of these, now 'called emphatically man,' presented himself to us here at Cambridge in the autumn of 1883. I

looked forward to many more pleasant messages
from my old friend, if not pleasant meetings with
him, when, a few months later, the sad intelligence
arrived which closed all such prospects.

"I put these facts and dates together in order to
show what degree of intimacy I had with Calverley.
As undergraduates we lived pretty near each other,
saw each other almost every day in hall and chapel
and lecture-room, and contended together in examinations ; but for the greater part of those years we
were not intimate. My circle of acquaintance lay
chiefly outside Christ's, among old school-fellows or
the friends of my elder brother, who when I went
up had just taken his degree from Trinity. Calverley, on the other hand, seemed to find his set in
the College. He seemed disposed to lead a quiet life.
The shock he had received at Oxford had made
him resolve, I suppose, to put a curb on his wilder
instincts. But with his wildness some of his energy
seemed to be lost. Like the cat that passes its life
in dozing before the fire, he seemed to hold in
abeyance—and this was his characteristic ever after
—energies which could only find play in a wild state,

a spirit which could not be tame without becoming indolent as well. But the reputation he brought with him to Cambridge, and the charm of his character, made him, as a matter of course, the centre of attraction in the College. I do not think he laid himself out for anything of the kind, but the clever fellows gathered round him and lived in his rooms, which thus became the focus of all the sociability of the place. At all this in the beginning I looked on from a distance ; but by the time that Calverley and I were in our third year, and began to look down upon a host of juniors, when Skeat, Sendall, Hales, Walter Besant, Peile and others had entered the College, I had approached nearer to Calverley's set and was on more familiar terms with him, though even then we were not exactly intimate. But society in a University is subject to an annual transformation. The men of 1856 were dispersed to the four winds, and Calverley, as candidate for a Fellowship, was left behind ; then went the men of 1857, and I was left behind. Thus we were thrown together in the end—first as the only representatives left of a certain college generation, and still more afterwards as the two junior Fellows of Christ's.

"Then first we became real friends. I soon felt the peculiar fascination that he exerted upon every-one. Being both alike classical men, we had a good many topics in common. We showed each other the translations we made from Greek poets ; we talked about Tennyson. We often spent the afternoons together at the racquet-court, and if we returned home too late for hall, we would dine together at his rooms or mine and afterwards spend the evening together. It was a pleasant time, and I have often thought of it since.

"But it came to an end ; and when some time later we found ourselves again near enough to each other in London to renew the old intercourse, the habit was broken. It was always delightful to me to meet him, and we met not unfrequently between 1863 and 1869. I can call to mind many evenings spent in his company and some long rambles that we made together in London streets and Hampstead lanes. But the Cambridge days between 1857 and 1861 were the only period during which I lived in unbroken intimacy with him. It was then I formed the idea of him which now lives and will always live in my mind. I took my farewell of him (unconsciously) in a long walk from Grasmere up Dunmail Raise in the summer of 1875: at least, I cannot recollect that I ever saw him after that time.

"When I look back I see that his character proved, when I came to know him well, more interesting and more uncommon than I had imagined it when I knew him but slightly. I had thought of him as only the regulation prodigy of undergraduates, and I found him to be infinitely more than that. He was not merely one of those young fellows who can do equally well whatever they turn their hand to, but who, fortunately for more ordinary people, are lazy, and though they can do great things, deliberately prefer to do little things or nothing. The first rumour we heard of him described him so. His high-jump, we heard, was wonderful; he could write most amusing squibs; but if you wanted graver aptitudes, his Latin verses were almost cleverer than his comic rhymes, and he would certainly be the first or among the first men of his year, if only he could be induced to take a little trouble. Now all this that we heard was perfectly true. It was not even, as in the case of nine out of ten University prodigies it is, exaggerated. His rhymes have passed far beyond the University public, are known to thousands after twenty years, and seem likely to live as long as Praed's. His Latin verses are not only clever, but in their way quite a wonder. Nor did he break down in the Senate House, but actually maintained his reputation for scholarship without forfeiting his reputation for laziness. And no one who knew him can doubt that he had a fund of other gifts which he had never an opportunity of using, and that he could have excited admiration in other circumstances in quite other ways. That kind of phœnix that we meet with so often in sensational novels is no doubt impossible; such all-accomplished, invincible persons are not found in real life; but persons do appear surprising enough to suggest these impossible imaginations, and Calverley was one of them. He was clever in every way; whatever he did showed cleverness; and at

one or two points he was wonderful. At the same
time he was very indolent; and an indolent man
cannot, as the novelist would have us think, possess
universal and accurate knowledge. Calverley, no
doubt, gave the impression that if he cared to do so
he could acquire almost any kind of knowledge
rapidly; but he did not care to do it, and accordingly
his stock of acquired knowledge was at that time
not at all remarkable.

"Any one who came expecting merely to see a
prodigy might for a moment be disappointed, but
the next moment he would discover that he had
before him something much better and more interesting than a prodigy. The phœnix of novelists,
if he appeared in real life, would be simply a
humbug, simply an ambitious pretender, keeping
up with great contrivance and labour an appearance of more knowledge than he really had. Now
there never was a man more unpretending, more
unambitious than Calverley. Instead of uttering
oracles, or trying to stand up to specialists on their
own ground, he usually professed, with perfect
simplicity, when the conversation demanded special

knowledge, to have no such knowledge. His modesty
was almost exaggerated. With a kind of humorous
frankness he stood before the world, in those days, as
he stands in his poems, a merry happy fellow who
knows just what he has been taught at school and
whom nobody will suspect of knowing more. He
did know a great deal more. He had a good
healthy memory, to which verses that took his fancy
readily stuck ; he knew his Virgil with the same
thorough familiarity with which many men of his
generation knew their Tennyson. Still I do not
think he had that almost morbid trick of remembering
which has helped many a 'prodigy' to keep up an
appearance of universal knowledge. It was not his
way to astonish the company by producing out of the
store of his memory some piece of knowledge that he
was not expected to possess. Nor did he give himself much trouble even to sustain his character as a
wit. The University of Cambridge in old times used
to have a professional wit who was called the Tripos,
from the three-legged stool—so I learn from Mr.
Wordsworth—on which he used to sit on public
occasions ; a trace of his function still appears in

the copy of comic verses which annually appear along with the honour lists and which being called from him Tripos verses have now transferred his name to the honour lists themselves. As Calverley wrote the best copy of Tripos verses extant, so we may say that he was in his time, in all but the three-legged stool, the Tripos of the University in the old sense of the word. He was the wit, the jester, whose jokes were repeated through the whole University and who also became, as it were, the official father of all foundling jokes. Persons, therefore, who came to his rooms came to hear jokes and to carry them away. It would not have been surprising, nay, it would have seemed almost a matter of course, if the consciousness of sustaining this part had made him somewhat artificial, if there had been something studied in his conversation, if the jokes when they came had now and then betrayed a little preparation or carried a faint smell of the midnight oil. But, again, never was there a man more free from such consciousness, such artifice, than Calverley. I should say he never asked himself the question how he appeared to his

company or whether he was sustaining successfully
his reputation as a wit.   Accordingly, though good
jokes were by no means wanting, yet there was no   •
incessant scintillation; and a visitor who had heard
of him as a wit, and came to pick up good sayings,
might chance to be disappointed, when he found a
perfectly unaffected, rational person, who could talk
for a long time without betraying anything more
remarkable than that he certainly took a light-
hearted view of life.

"It took a longer acquaintance to recognize the
humourist.   Gradually through all the Latin verses,
the squibs, the conversational jokes, and the practical
jokes, you began to see something more than mere
vivacity, namely, an original vein of humour.   He
took an odd, a queer view of life ; he saw everything in an unusual light; but he saw things really
so, could not see them otherwise, and the same
eccentricity which gives their flavour to his writings
influenced his actions and his whole course of life in
a most serious manner.

"His favourite writer seemed to me to be
Thackeray, and I could understand that it should

be so. He resembled Thackeray in having not
merely a keen sense of the ridiculous, but also
what I may call a comic philosophy of life. Only,
this philosophy was much lighter and more fantastic
in him than in Thackeray. He had the same perception of the pompous hollowness of the ways of
men, but there was neither bitterness nor seriousness
in his perception. He could not, like Thackeray,
preach or moralize on the subject, nor could he even
be at the trouble to produce a continuous satire. He
is a caricaturist rather than a satirist. Nevertheless his comedy has generality in it. What he finds
ridiculous is not this thing or that thing, but the ways
of men in general. His laughter has not merely
boyish glee but elvish mockery, and his motto might
be the exclamation of Puck, 'Lord! what fools these
mortals be!' I do not know whether the thousands
who now know and quote his witty rhymes perceive
this quality in them; perhaps they will think I refine
too much. But those who knew Calverley know that
his humour lay actually in his character, that he is
not to be called a humourist because he wrote
humorously, but that he could not help writing

humorously because he was a humourist. And
evidently every poem of his harps on the same
string. That boy 'whom his familiar friends call
Tommy' and who 'was what nurses call a *limb*'
appears in all of them, though in most he has ceased
to be a boy. He appears as a freshman, as a brief-
less barrister with 'a distant prospect of making a
fortune,' as a lover; he has always the same inimitable pose, the same way of speaking. Well!
we knew this person. Many a time have I walked
down Petty Cury and Regent Street with him, and
noted the glee with which he entered into everything. In every street he seemed to see a picture
by Leech. What is it Walt Whitman says?—

O, all ye men and women walking about in ordinary costume,
How *curious* you seem to me, and how I love you all!

"To Calverley they seemed curious, but also ridiculous! At least their airs of decorum and respecta-
bility seemed to him intolerably absurd. He chafed,
as he walked along, at every formal gesture, at
every conventional simper, and sometimes his spleen
showed itself in madcap pranks. Meanwhile he
treasured up, as Leech himself might have done,

every grimace of roguish impudence on the face of a street urchin.

"An absolute rebellion against rule, as of some wild creature or some Robin Goodfellow, is the humour of Calverley. At school he cannot put up with the masters and the lessons. They are really too absurd! At College it is the Dons, the Chapels, the College discipline. But he enters into and enjoys much of what he ridicules. That is what makes him such a consummate parodist. He has a natural talent for language and a remarkable sense of rhythm. At school he has had to write a great many Latin verses, and has been led to think much about diction and literary style. All this was much to his taste. He assimilated Virgil in a wonderful manner, and if anything among the products of human civilization seemed to him really admirable, or excited a feeling of genuine reverence, I suppose it was Virgil's poetry. But even poetry and literature, however much he enjoys them, fall at last under the ban of his uncontrollable humour. When he has mastered all metrical forms, all delicacies of poetic diction, the elvish mood comes on him again.

' Lord ! what fools these mortals be !' he thinks,
and sets himself to show what modern word-painting
can make of the St. John's Wood omnibus, and utters
a lofty apostrophe, with ' tears in the voice,' to the
Beadles of the Burlington Arcade. Even Virgil
does not escape. In the Tripos verses we seem to
see the divine poet gone mad, and it produces the
strangest feeling to find all those inimitable, almost
sacred, refinements of language so ingeniously mis-
applied.

"But the elvish character lay so deep in Calverley
that he could not in the least control it. He was
always resorting to the practical joke, as the many
stories current about him testify. Nevertheless, as
far as I know, his practical jokes were always of the
innocent kind, and such as could injure no one but
himself. Almost the first time I ever met him in
society, when we were both freshmen, was at a grand
gathering at the Lodge at Christ's. Many of the
great Dons, the Whewells and Sedgwicks of that day,
had been dining with the Master, and in the evening
the drawing-room was thrown open to younger
people, among whom were some undergraduates.

There was music, and in due time Calverley was
seated at the piano giving us an Italian song. Soon
a murmur passed among us undergraduates that his
Italian was purely fictitious. So it was. Just as
in one of his parodies, there were all the recognized
forms of art, but if you listened attentively you
found the song a mere string of nonsense, made up
of some dozen Italian words that every Englishman
knows,—contralto, sotto voce, impresario, &c. This
makes but a poor story, though indeed the cool
assurance of the young impostor in the midst of that
rather pompous assemblage was really laughable.
But it affords a specimen of his practical jokes,
which were only sudden outbreaks of uncontrollable
mutiny against everything formal or conventional.
They were perfectly harmless to other people, but
they were not always harmless to himself. It was a
misfortune that, with this irrepressible propensity, he
had to spend so many years in an ancient College,
where he was expected to conform to a routine
more formal than that of ordinary life, and where,
after he ceased to be an undergraduate, he found
not enough of incident or occupation to reconcile

him to the monotony. His marriage and migration
to London came opportunely to rouse him out of a
condition which was unprofitable, and was beginning to deserve the name of sloth.

"In truth, the routine of a college could produce
no other effect upon such a temperament. To
call out the wonderful powers that were dormant
in him, a more interesting mode of life, more variety
and adventure, were needed. The chapel-bell
stupefied him. I come back to my comparison of
the cat snoozing before the fireplace. I have seen
somewhere a description of La Fontaine, which
represents him as nursing all his life a silent grudge
against Louis XIV. and his civilization, as cherishing
within him the old 'esprit gaulois' and watching with
'sullen irony and desperate resignation' all the
pompous routine of Court, Academy, and Salon.
Yet he said nothing and made himself a favourite
in that artificial society ; the wild creature became
a sleek, sleepy, domestic pet. Does not his epitaph
betray the secret?—

> Jean s'en alla comme il était venu,
> Mangea le fonds avec le revenu,

Tint les trésors chose peu nécessaire.
Quant à son temps, bien sut le dispenser:
Deux parts en fit, dont il soulait passer
L'une à dormir, et l'autre à ne rien faire.

" Those last four lines are not inappropriate to Calverley as he was at that time.

" Many of his friends have testified that his character had a serious side, of which you became aware on closer acquaintance. I can quite conceive this, for never was there a character more rational, more unaffected. His very humour was but a kind of sincerity, a child-like simplicity pushed to excess. His mind and imagination also were pure. It was only natural that such a character should acquire a fund of seriousness as life itself became serious, and in particular after he made his very happy marriage. But in those later days it was not my fortune to see him very often. He comes before me as he was a quarter of a century ago, light-hearted, enjoying life from the moment he rose to the moment when he went to sleep, not noisy or foolish in his mirth, but almost always mirthful. I think I never knew a man who was

such pleasant company, for he was quite free from
vanity or any kind of self-consciousness, quite free
also from every kind of unreasonableness or angu-
larity. With all that irrepressible freedom there
was nothing harsh, but the most genuine good-
fellowship, and—I was going to say, good temper,
but the word seems poor indeed to describe that
mixture of joyousness and sweetness!

"But I suspect he had also a talent for action,
which was not only little known, but which remained
undeveloped. His face and figure were not those
of a poet or artist ; and I well remember that when,
as a freshman at Christ's, I had just heard of him,
and of his wonderful qualities, and tried to pick him
out by guess among the faces at the freshmen's
table, I went quite wrong. He looked rather like
the typical English hero—a solid muscular body, a
face full of animal spirits, careless good-humour,
and frolicsome daring. But there was no ambition
in it, there was the misfortune! He was a hero
asleep! If Nature commonly, where she gives
powers, gives also the restless desire to use them,
she had departed from her rule in this instance.

Only some great need would ever have drawn him from his tent. And it was his lot to saunter along the high road of life, where the cases do not arise which call for such powers as his. We boast sometimes—I wish I could think with justice—that Englishmen spring up wherever they are wanted capable of ruling, of conquering, of mastering difficulties. One of such Englishmen, who never was wanted, I shall always suppose Calverley to have been.

" As I lay down the pen, the recollection of that last walk up Dunmail Raise comes iupon me. I remember the last flash of his elvish humour. We told each other what we had been doing in a literary way. I asked him, did he ever write reviews ? He had done so occasionally, he answered. He knew an editor, who occasionally sent him new editions of classical authors for review. He had lately reviewed an edition of Ovid's Heroïdes. On the line, ' Nil mihi rescribas : attamen ipse veni !' he had objected to *attamen* as evidently a false reading. Why *attamen !* He suspected that some term of endearment was concealed under it. He would

1.   I

suggest *attagen!* 'O you duck! come yourself.' That the *e* in *attagen* was long was no sufficient objection to this conjecture; for the case here was vocative! 'To my amazement,' he said, 'the editor actually printed all this!'

'Lord! what fools these mortals be!'"

As the reader already knows, Calverley has been taken from us in the very prime of his manhood. At what period were sown the seeds of that cruel and treacherous malady[1] which ultimately caused his death, can now only be matter of conjecture. All that can be stated with certainty is, that long before the end came—how long it is impossible to say—he had been suffering from its unknown and unsuspected presence.

For some years his health had been gradually declining; and though his mental powers remained almost to the last intrinsically bright and clear, and the charm of his society never ceased to delight the few of us who had opportunities of enjoying it —such opportunities grew year by year rarer and

[1] He died of Bright's disease.

rarer, giving place to intervals of physical uneasiness and mental depression, which slowly led to his more and more complete withdrawal from work and from the world. When at length the hopeless and incurable character of his disorder became fully apparent, his affectionate nature busied itself almost exclusively with thoughts of those whom he was leaving behind. A few short days before his death, in a conversation with myself about the future of his boys, his mind suddenly recurring to those fields of classic lore from which it was never long absent, he exclaimed, in tones rendered more pathetic by an increasing difficulty of utterance,—

ὦ παῖ, γένοιο πατρὸς εὐτυχέστερος·

In their name we may accept, and reverently repeat the aspiration embodied in this line, but we may surely also complete the prayer, by adding, τὰ δ' ἄλλ' ὅμοιος !²

To pass through life, if so it may be, untouched by the shadow of that melancholy destiny, which clouded his days and brought his years to an end

¹ Sophocles, Ajax, l. 550. ² Id. Ibid. l. 551.

as a tale that is told; not hoping, for that may hardly be, to rival him in powers of mind and intellect; but in other respects—in manliness and native worth, in truthfulness, uprightness, and simplicity of character—to be even such as he was!

He died on Sunday, the 17th of February, and was buried in the cemetery at Folkestone, by the side of his infant daughter, laid there sixteen years before. He had always liked the place, with its breezy heights, and sunny slopes, and exhilarating air; and on the morning of the Saturday following his death, we took him there. And there we left him.

> " And in our ears, till hearing dies,
>   One set slow bell will seem to toll
>   The passing of the sweetest soul
> That ever looked with human eyes."
>
> TENNYSON : *In Memoriam.*

" *It was not, to restore thy flickering breath,*
  Or hold thee back, just nearing towards the Light,
  But—whilst that Sun of Life, whom we name Death,
  Rose on thy closing, or thy opening sight—
  To catch some whisper of thy new delight,
  Some earnest of thy fainting soul's surprise,
  And see the radiance quickening through the veil
  Of palsied speech and leaden-lidded eyes,—
  That we, bright Spirit! who stood and watched thee fail
  And sink, and pass through gloom and utter night,
  One instant, and no more, would fain have stayed thy flight!"

W. J. S.

LUPUS ET CANIS.

MAXIMA pars hominum vitio versatur eodem,
   Qui quærunt sibi nil aliud, quam cingere luxu
Sese, et divitiis : auro famam, decus, ipsas
Permutant vitas. " An ero locupletior," aiunt,
" Servus ?" " Eris." " Bene habet," respondent,
     " servus ero. Quid ?
" Esse velim liber ; libertate at melior res."

   Horum uti sermones volvo, mihi fabula quædam,
Nota quidem, in mentem venit; at, ne te morer,
     audi.

   In quadam fuit urbe Canis ; Canis inclytus, acer,
Atque domus custos locupletis. Viderat illum
Forte lupus, macer esurie, visumque salutat.
" Qui fit, amice," rogat—cupido ut miratur ocello
Corporis et decus et molem, perpastaque membra,—
" Qui fit ita ut niteas ? Longe qui fortior, ipse

" Impastus nemora hæc noctuque dieque peragro."

Cui Canis arridens : " Vin nostris moribus uti ?

" Elige, namque potes."   " Qui possum," ait, " oh

    bone ?   Nam sum

" Aspera passus multa : cibi expers atque soporis

" Montivagum caput et nivibus pulsatur et imbri ;

" Dic modo, quid faciam."   " Domus est servanda :

    latrones

" Arcendi a foribus."   " Sum plane," ait ille, " pa-

    ratus,

   " Idque libenter agam."   Quid plura ? utrique

    placebat

Propositum, et comites peragunt iter, ipsaque tan-

    gunt

Mœnia, cum subito aspexit detrita catena

Colla lupus socii.   " Quidnam hoc," ait ?   " Est

    nihil."   " At tu

" Dic mihi, dic quæso."   " Sum nempe ferocior,"

    inquit,

" Utquo vigil sim nocte, quiescam luce, catena

" Alligor : at nihil est : gratus sopor iste diurnus ;

" Vespere ubique vagor, nullo retinente, per agros,

" Frusta mihi domino lautæque obsonia mensæ

" Per totam præbente diem ; Sic absque labore

" Vita beata fugit."   " Si vis tamen effugere is-
    stinc,

" Num potes arbitrio ? "   " Sane non id licet,"
    inquit.

" Verum itaque est ?   Equidem non tecum vivere
    tali

" Conditione volo : tu, re meliore potitus,

 'Utere sorte tua, ac valeas ! me libera semper

" Arva juvant : nocet empta jugo, mihi crede, vo-
    luptas."

        July 4th, 1848.

HYMN TO THE MORNING.   (COLERIDGE.)

(Written in the Vale of Chamouni.)

AWAKE my soul! not only passive praise
   Thou owest! not alone these swelling tears,
Mute thanks and secret ecstasy!   Awake,
Voice of sweet song!   Awake, my heart, awake!
Green vales and icy cliffs, all join my song!
   Thou first and chief, sole sovran of the Vale!
O struggling with the darkness all the night,
And visited all night by troops of stars,
Or when they climb the sky or when they sink:
Companion of the morning star at dawn,
Thyself Earth's rosy star, and of the dawn
Co-herald: wake, O wake, and utter praise!
Who sank thy sunless pillars deep in earth?
Who filled thy countenance with rosy light?
Who made thee parent of perpetual streams?

IDEM LATINE REDDITUM.

RUMPE moras, mea mens! non tantum laudibus
istis
Nunc opus! haud lacrymis satis est turgescere, cæca
Fervere lætitia, ac tacitas persolvere grates:
Excute, cor, somnos! vosque adspirate canenti
Gramineæ valles, glacieque rigentia saxa!
Incipe, vox arguta, melos!

Te, maxime regum,
Te primum aggredior, vallis decus: humida cujus
Nox caput invadit tenebris; quem plurima longas
Sidera per noctes, nunc sero orientia cælo,
Nunc obitura, petunt: rosei qui sideris instar,
Luciferi comes ipse, diem lucemque reportas,
Surge age, rumpe moras, laudesque effunde solutas!
Quis tua, quis solida posuit fundamina terra,
Sol ubi semper abest? roseo quis lumine tingens
Vultum fluminea fecit te prole parentem?

And you, ye five wild torrents fiercely glad!
Who called you forth from night and utter death,
From dark and icy caverns called you forth,
Down those precipitous, black, jagged Rocks,
For ever shattered and the same for ever?
Who gave you your invulnerable life,
Your strength, your speed, your fury, and your
      joy,
Unceasing thunder, and eternal foam?
And who commanded—and the silence came—
" Here let the billows stiffen, and have rest?"

   Ye icefalls! ye that from the mountain's brow
Adown enormous ravines slope amain—
Torrents, methinks, that heard a mighty voice,
And stopped at once amid their maddest plunge—
Motionless torrents! silent cataracts!
Who made you glorious as the gates of Heaven
Beneath the keen full moon?   Who bade the sun
Clothe you with rainbows?   Who with living
     flowers
Of loveliest blue, spread garlands at your feet?
God! let the torrents, like a shout of nations,
Answer! and let the ice plains echo, God!

Vos etiam, quini qui flumina volvitis amnes

Turbida lætitia! quis vos a noctis acerba

Sede, quis exitio, gelidisque excivit ab antris,

Præcipites inter scopulos, et scrupea saxa

Ire jubens, loca perpetua collapsa ruina?

Quis vobis nullo violandam **vulnere** vitam

Lætitiamque alasque dedit? vis unde, furorque,

Spumæque insomnes, ac fulmina nescia sisti?

Quis pelago dixit—subeuntque silentia dicto—

" Hic tumidi rigeant fluctus; hic unda quiescat?"

    Lympha gelu constricta! fero quæ vertice montis

Devolvis rigidos per saxa horrentia fluctus—

Quamque equidem voces credo agnovisse Potentis,

Et fremitum, atque omnem subito frænasse furo-

      rem—

O tacitæ decursus aquæ! O sine gurgite torrens!

Quis vobis fulgore dedit splendescere, quali

Sidereæ portæ, plenæ sub frigora lunæ?

Unde, precor, jussus vestras Sol Iride picta

Vestit aquas? qua serta manu funduntur, et una

Cærulei flores, vivum decus? Est Deus, alto

Torrentes clamore fremant, voxque insonet ingens,

Gentis opus! vos arva gelu torrentia, plena

God! sing, ye meadow streams, with gladsome voice!

Ye pine-groves, with your soft and soul-like
    sounds!

And they, too, have a voice, yon piles of snow,

And in their perilous fall shall thunder, God!

Reddite voce, "Deum!" vos prata recentia rivis,
Et pineta sacrum foliis spirantia murmur;
Hæc quoque, namque licet, nivea quæ mole laborant
Saxa " Deum!" vasto revoluta a monte sonabunt.

September 27th, 1848.

ROLL ON, THOU DEEP AND DARK BLUE
OCEAN, ROLL!

VOLVERE, cæruleis fundoque carentibus undis!
    Volvere! regna virum tua littora: regna,
        quibus nil,
Te præter, superesse ætas dedit.   O ubi Persis
Assyriæque vetus sedes? ubi Græcia, et ingens
Gloria Romulidum?   Sopor urget ferreus omnes,
Omnes deperiere.   Manes immobilis, idem,
Tu, vitreis immensus aquis, nescisque reverti
Ponte! tot humanos quanquam miscerier æstus
Vidisti, tot sceptra retro, tot prælia ferri—
Nullæ in fronte minæ: liquido sed molle susurro
Labere qualis eras primi sub origine mundi,
Qualis in æternum labere volubilis ævum.
    1850.

MAGNAS artis opes, manibusque imitabile nostris
    Naturæ decus, et partos sine Marte triumphos,
Aggredior cantare.   Juvat revocasse parentum
Umbras, et simulacra modis splendentia miris
Exiguâ in tabulâ : juvat ardua cernere templa,
Æstivumque nemus, fontesque et picta Lyæo
Culta, vel ingentes hominum mirarier urbes.
Apparet lapsura novâ nece Troja, ducesque
Argolici ; salit ecce ferox Romanus in hostem,
Et desolatas rursum aspectamus Athenas.
Non aliter persæpe trahunt sublustria sensus
Somnia sopitos, et imagine ludimur aureâ :
Delinita tument dum pectora, voxque volentum
Dicere abest ; at mira, novâ dulcedine captas,
Religio superat mentes, fruimurque priorum
Colloquio, immemoresque loci raptamur, et horæ.

    I.   K

Cernis ut immensâ se mole attollat in auras,
Ædes inter humo æquatas, avulsaque saxis
Saxa, Coliseum ?   Sanctâ sub rupe morari
Musa jubet, sæclique animos revocare sepulti,
Astra ruinosas spectant ubi conscia turres,
Et campos ubi Roma fuit.   Sic omnia pictor
Rite memor servavit, inenarrabile pingens
Dextrâ opus, ac tabulæ dans vitam ac verba silenti.

Hic vero instructas acie, medioque phalanges
Marte, vel in crasso revolutos pulvere currus,
Formarit, non arte rudis ; piceumque colorem
Addidit, ac multâ texit formidine campum.
Ille canes, pecudumque laborantisque coloni
Pinxit opus, fecitque boves per prata vagari,
Serpere de sylvis fumum, aut sub margine rivi
Ludere ridentes pueros : aliusque domorum
Arcanos penetrat thalamos, vigilemque sub altâ
Nocte senem jussit visu ardescente tueri
Argenti gazas, aurique talenta reposti.
Atque alius sacri profert miracula Libri,
Pastoris laudes, debellatumque gigantem,
Aut casum Babylonis, aquas ubi propter, inani
Fletu indulgebant, noctis per tædia longæ,

Isacidæ.   Atque alius supremi arcana reclusit
Luminis, instantemque Deum, trepidosque sub ipsis
Tartareis stantes portis denso agmine manes.
Nulli fas illis mortali excedere tectis.
Sed ne quære prius, quæ nocte teguntur acerbâ,
Neu scrutare Deum.   Nobis sat pandere multæ
Artis iter, quocunque ferat sacrata voluptas,
Concessamque viam cœli affectare futuri.

    1850.

ATLANTEA feror trans æquora, transque so-
    norum
Nimbis Ionium, pastoralesque recessus
Arcadiæ: apparent candentia marmore saxa,
Prataque olivifera, et rivorum argenteus error,
Speluncæque, lacusque, et densi palmite clivi.
Hæ tibi divitiæ, musis gratissima tellus,
Attica! quas Asiæ frustrà Libyæque colonus
Optat, et auratis Hermus mercetur arenis.
Non mirum veteres hæc fortunata locorum
Nobiliore choro, formisque implesse pöetas
Ætheriis; ipsa aura Deum spirare videtur,
Nec mortale melos ad littora volvere fluctus.
Ergo cuique jugo data numina, quâque sub umbrâ
Surrexere aræ: tum parva sacraria nasci,

[1] Chancellor's Prize Poem, Oxford, 1851.

Tum variæ paulatim artes.   Didicero colorem
Saxa pati, nec fronde suâ turgescere marmor,
Et sylvæ niveis interlucere columnis.

   Sed non lucorum tenebras artisque vetustæ
Prisca rudimenta, et latitantia numina sylvis,
Fert animus lustrare: vocant distantis Hymetti
Culmina, et assiduis decertans Sunion undis
Piniferum ostentat gremium camposque patentes.
Quippe hinc torva domus, desolatumque videri
Palladis armatæ solium, clypeataque quondam
Effigies; hinc hasta tremens, galeæque coruscus
Apparebat apex, et rubræ in vertice cristæ.[1]
Illas sæpe vagans Ægæo in marmore nauta,
Cum nimbi posuere, jubarque orientis Eoi
Trans Œtæa procul splendet juga, vidit apertâ
Luce coruscantes, et remo innixus inerti
Substitit, optatas ut compellaret Athenas.

[1] Soph. Aj., 1217.

> " γενοίμαν ἵν' ὑλᾶεν ἔπεστι πόντου
> πρόβλημ' ἁλίκλυστον, ἄκραν
> ὑπὸ πλάκα Σουνίου,
> τὰς ἱερὰς ὅπως
> προσείποιμεν Ἀθάνας."

Namque ubi convulsam hanc molem, postesque
    tueris
Avulso capite, et longæ data saxa ruinæ ;
Stabat aprico ædes de marmore, candida partim,
Partim cæruleos cæli mentita colores,
Gaudebatque die, et sese pandebat ad ortus
Luminis, equo jugis magnam spectabat in urbem.
Quales aeriis in cautibus Apennini,
Aut nimbis involvit ubi latera ardua Parnes,
Suspendere domos aquilæ, plenoque tuentur
Solem oculo, nidosque fovent ingentibus alis.
Flore coronati postes, sertisque superbi
Auricomis ; variâ lucebat tænia guttâ,[1]
Mæandroque frequens circùm color ibat amæno.
Quos supra, testata truces ancilia pugnas
Ordine pendebant tereti, cælataque in auro
Nomina, magnorum monumenta et munus avorum.

Necnon et variâ signarat imagine frontem
Artificis manus, et lateri cælarat honores.

---

[1] *Vide* Wordsworth's " Greece," description of the Metopes,
Triglyphs, &c., round the Parthenon, guttæ, festoons, and
golden shields.

Hic Centaurorum rabiem Lapitheiaque arma
Aspiceres, trepidasque **nurus**, et Thesea **raptis**
Mensarum exuviis non irrita bella moventem.[1]
Illic in lucem matri non debita Pallas,[2]
Arma tenens, surgebat : eam chorus omnis Olympi
Spectabat, sobolemque pater lætatus ab alto
Veram agnoscebat solio, juxtàque locabat.
Circùm antiqua Ceres, Cythereaque, Mercuriusque,
Mulciber innixus ferro, Victoriaque alis
Ardua; nec virides texere Hyperiona fluctus,
Nec pallente Erebi latuit Proserpina luco.
Contra respondit tellus percussa tridenti,[3]
Et sonipes, et sylva tumens, lymphæque sequaces,
Ardentesque Deum facies.   Ibi regia Virgo,
Neptunusque pater, neque adhuc data victima
   Phœbo
Leucothea, et vitreis in curribus Amphitrite,
Herseque, Aglaurosque, et semper inops Erisicthon.
Hæc inter tranquilla maris lucebat imago,

[1] Library of Entert. Knowledge, British Museum, p. 139.
" Metopes."
[2] E. Pediment, p. 237.
[3] W. Pediment, p. 247.

Vivaque Callirhöe, gelidâque Ilissus in umbrâ,
Et nascens Erycina, fretis acclinis eburnis.
Talibus ingentem divæ splendoribus arcem
Phidiacus labor ornavit, saxoque caduco
Immortale dedit decus, et sacravit in ævum.

Quanquam, o magno parens artis, cui sculptile
    marmor,
Cui niveum parebat ebur, gazæque liquentes
Amnis Mæonii ; nunc o si regna revisas
Patria, dilectamque iterum spectaveris urbem,
Urbem reginam non amplius !   Exulat oris
Spirans saxum aliis, pulchri fugere colores :
Te quoque, divinæ domus ægidis, alter Ulixes[1]
Polluit ; alter, agens rubrum ipsa in limina martem,
Avulsit prædam mediis altaribus Ajax ;[2]
Quot tua funeribus nutarint saxa, quot iras
Certantum populorum, et belli incendia norint,
Testatur via clausa situ, stratæque deorum
Effigies, portæque feris hyemique patentes.

[1] Demetrius Poliorcetes.   (Vide Æn. i. 40, ii. 404.)
[2] Sylla dragged Aristion from the altar.   Brit. Mus. p. 56.
(Vide Æn. ii. 164.)

Scilicet hanc ædem Venetorum, ac turbida Sullæ
Agmina vastarunt; hanc audivere cadentem,
Sulphuris impulsu Scythici,[1] Cephissides undæ,
Æginæque latus niveum, distansque Caphareus.
Illa nocte greges nemorosi ex arce Lycæi
Pastor agens, miro splendore rubescere cœlum
Vidit, et ex adytis non thurea nubila ferri.
Vidit, et intremuit: paucisque volantibus horis,
Templum ingens quà stabat, erat cæmenta tueri,
Et tetros cineres, caligantemque ruinam.

Atqui sæpe, cavum quo tempore sidera saxum
Frigida perspiciunt, quo rerum apparet imago
Maxima, densatæque cadunt è postibus umbræ;
Desertis juvat ire jugis, aulâque vagari
Sub vacuâ, et pronis in casum hærere columnis.
Infrà reliquias urbis, prostrataque passim
Templa vides, murosque; vides, Jovis atria quon-
    dam,
Fragmina, Mavortisque jugum, lapidesque theatri:—
At circa loca mille, decus confessa parentum,

[1] The Turks set fire to some gunpowder which the Vene-
tians had left in the temple.   Encycl. Brit. "Athens."

Scena nitent varia : hic Salamis se tollit ab undis
Contemptorem Asiæ, Marathonis littora longè,
Portaque Thebarum apparet, materque Pelasgæ
Ascra lyræ ; propior, sylvis aperitur Eleusin
In mediis, ac nigra quatit pineta Cithæron.
Tum flagrare faces in pectore, voxque volenti
Dicere abest ; sensusque haurit diffusa per omnes
Conscia fama loci, lapsas revocamur in horas,
Et venit in mentem, quorum cinis abditur infrà.

At postquam adventum, paries ubi texit opacus
Thesauros adytumque deæ, senisque columnis
Interclusa domus ; tum vultum atque ora parentum
Fas ipsa aspicere, et vivis miscerier umbris.
Namque hic[1] ingentem cætum, matresque, virosque,
Effusos ad sacra, senes, pallisque puellas
Extuderat longis opifex : quæ pocula ferrent,
Quæque faces, calathosque ; alias umbracula soli
Pandere, vel sacri miratas pondera pepli.[2]
Has ad pacatæ tendentes Palladis arcem
Turba sequebatur taurorum, et debita morti

[1] The Panathenaic frieze. Libr. Brit. Mus. p. 182, &c.
[2] Slabs. No. 17-25.

Corpora : pars longo mugitu et fronte reluctans
Terribili ; tacitâ pars majestate superbos
Volvit ovans gressus, collique volumina in arcum
Colligit, imbelles ultrò comitata magistros.
Proxima, queis gracilis testudo aut tibia curæ,
Sortiti loca, queisque merum tutarier urnis ;
Et velata silens capiebat dona sacerdos.[1]

Ast[2] aliâ de parte citas ardere quadrigas
Fecerat, et pubem tunicatam, ardentiaque ossa
Bellatoris equi ; quem, dorso immotus, habenis
Flexit inauratis eques, instantemque retorsit.
Ollis dissimiles habitus, grandisve cothurnus,
Aut lænæ undantes, aut Arcadis umbra galeri :
Atque alius[3] tunicam et gemmati pondera baltei
Nectit ovans, lauruque caput circumdat equinum,
Victricemque alius[4] meritâ cervice coronam
Accipit, aut, segnes gestu exhortatus[5] amicos,
Prona rapit spatia, et campo decurrit aperto.

[1] Nos. 84-90.
[2] Nos. 26-81.   *Vide* Libr. Brit. Mus. p. 165, &c.
[3] No. 46.   [4] Slab, No. 26.   [5] No. 47.

Nec minus intereâ motus proceraque membra
Ipsorum mirabere equûm ; mirabere nares
Fulmineas, et crura modis luctantia miris,
Luminaque, osque fremens, et stantes sanguine
    venas.
Partem, indignantum similem, certare videres
Arrectos in frena, jubasque atque agmina caudæ
Excutere, et celsas in frontes cogere martem.[1]
Stare loco partem,[2] notamque micantibus escam
Auribus accipere,[3] aut gradientes agmine lento
Alternare pedem, plausove quiescere collo.
Talem Miltiades currum, talemve regebat
Armiger Automedon : tales invictus Achilles
Bello addebat equos, ubi Larissæa sub ipsis
Crista relucebat muris, flebantque Pelasgo
Hectora Trojanæ revolutum in pulvere matres.

  Quæ vero integris species, quæ gratia formis,
Artificisque manus quantam tractata per artem,
Tum sciat, avulsos lapides direptaque si quis
Fragmina post tanto videat, simulacraque vitâ
Fervida, vix summo simulacra exstantia saxo.

---

[1] Nos. 32, 34, 36, &c.   [2] No. 44, &c.   [3] No. 58.

Dicendum et peplus quales jactaret honores.
Illic arma Deum, debellatosque gigantas
Cernere erat, centumque manus sublime ferentem
Enceladum, et rapto pugnantem monte Typhoea.
Hunc Pandionio de semine plurima virgo
Neverat, hunc gemmis, hunc interseverat auro
Multiplicem, et pictis dederat splendere figuris.
Qualiter Assyrii cùm mercatoris ab alto
Effulgent vexilla mari, gaudentque colores
Ad solem reserare ; refert decora aureus æther,
Fictaque purpureis in fluctibus errat imago.
Talis erat species pepli lucentis aprico
Murice ; portantes pueri mollesque puellæ
Ad sonitum citharæ gradiuntur, et inclyta Divæ
Facta canunt.   Ut nocte satos Titanas, ut orbes
Gorgona sanguineos volventem, anguesque tri-
          lingues
Contuderit : tu, Diva, minas hominumque Deumque
Sprevisti pariter : Tityum testamur, et orsis
Vulcanum irrisis, pœnamque audacis Arachnes.
Te Larissæus juvenis, te novit amicam
Inachius Perseus ; tibi balsama Gallus, et Afer
Suppeditat, fusamque cremant Phœnices olivam.

Huc ades, O regina! tuis accingimur unà
Laudibus; et proprios nunquam obliviscere Graios!

    Sic divam orabant variâ prece.   Jamque sub
       ipsam
Portam adventantes, uno simul impete cuncti
Addunt in spatia, et laxis urgentur habenis.
Tum placidæ apparent facies, circàque sedentum
Ora immota Deum; Cereris tum apparet imago,
Latonæque genus duplex, et regia Juno:
Fulgida præ cunctis solium Tritonis eburnum
Pallas habet; non ense ferox, non ægida quassans,
Sed niveis radians vittis, risuque sereno.

    Talia per muros et per laquearia pictor
Atticus extuderat, gaudens revocare priorum
Gesta virum, ac tabulæ dare vitam et verba silenti.

    Quanquam, ædes formosa, tibi non signifer ordo
Parietis, aut fuco diversum marmor honores
Præcipuos tribuit: tali petat arte triumphos
Barbarus, audaci attollens super æthera nisu
Pyramidum moles, et splendida mausolea.

At tibi majestas, tibi simplex gratia formæ;
Te, dum cincta nites leviter spirantibus auris,
Et lucem simul ipsa refers, ipso æthere tractum
Visum ambire decus : circumque illustrior umbra,
Circum sancta quies, et non tua gloria fundi.
Religione novâ perculsi hæremus, et altè
Evehimur : nec tantus amor percurrere visu
Singula, quàm totâ paulisper imagine pasci
Ardescentem animum, dum sensus impleat omnes
Nec percepta prius, nec jam intellecta voluptas.

Teque, sub auspiciis cujus jussuque secundo
Templorum redivivus honos, artesque per orbem
Surrexere novæ ; te notâ in sede morantem
Fingit adhuc amor, et dulcem desiderat umbram.
Si non inscriptis titulos et nomina regum
Marte occisorum, vivit tua fama tropæis ;
Fulmina si vocis, quam mirabantur Athenæ,
Non sculpti servant lapides, non pagina chartæ ;
At patrii colles, at strata jacentibus aris
Pascua, perque altas templorum fragmina sylvas,
Te memorant, artemque tuam ; tibi vivida virtus
Clara dedit monumenta, et non mortale tropæum.

Jamque, licet vix ulla sibi monumenta **vetustas**
Servet adhuc, licet Italicis concesserit armis
Quisquis honos Graiorum, et nil nisi nominis umbram
Fas tanti superesse : manet tamen artis **avitæ**
Saltem aliquid ; manet illa patrum vestigia tardis
Passibus, et longo sectarier intervallo.
Forsitan et **nostris** aliquis spectarit in oris
Marmoreos apices, atque atria clausa columnis   .
Sole novo lucere ; ast illi irrepit imago
Arcis Palladiæ ; labuntur verba per aurem
Muta diu, Graiosque juvat meminisse parentes.

CAROLUS STUART BLAYDS.
e Coll. Balliol.

AUSTRALIA.[1]

INSULA Pacificis in fluctibus ilice multa
  Tecta jacet, pontumque jugis intercipit albis.
Supra nube vacans et nostro purior æther :
Ingentes intus campi, sectæque malignis
Tramitibus cautes, et ager non æquus aratro.
Hic ubi nunc lautas urbes, ubi rura juvenci
Fassa pedem, lætosque vides in collibus agnos ;
Barbara nuper ibi ducebat lampade luna
Gens incompositas inter querceta choreas,
Corporaque exuviis circumdabat atra ferinis.
Tantum auri vesana potest mutare cupido.

    Namque sub eluviem fluviorum et saxa repertum
Ingens pondus opum referunt : id fama per orbem
Detulit, ac resides populos accendit amore.
Huc Europææ gentes, huc Seres, et Indi
Convenere : novæ si quem telluris imago

    [1] University Prize Poem. Cambridge, 1853.

I.   L

Impulit, aut stimulis haud lenibus egit egestas.

Ut portum [1] tetigere rates, et, læta peracti
Æquoris, in terra graditur manus : ilicet ædes
Et vici apparent nivei,[2] simulataque priscæ
Anglia, et antiquo decoratæ more tabernæ.
Cernis equos, cernis currus ; partem Area, partem
Scena trahit, magnumque forum, circusque theatri ;
Et cuidam nemorum lustranti devia Lugens [3]
Monstratur Sinus ; hic patriis e finibus exsul
Plurimus inviso terram tractabat aratro,
Fœcundumque solum pœnis, et non sua rura.
Credas littus adhuc tracta stridere catena ;
Sed fuit.   Aversus petis urbem, et singula lustras ;
Præpes in æquoreas dum sol immittitur undas,
Tranquillumque nitent sub eburna carbasa luna.

Tu vero, desiderium cui suaserit ingens
Explorare sinum terræ, et rem quærere dextra,
Assurgis dum mane novum, dum flatus ab undis
Acrior, et lanæ percurrunt vellera cælum.
Tum tauros traheamque pares : huc arma ferantur,

[1] *Portum*, sc. Port Jackson, town of Sydney.
[2] *Nivei*, the buildings being of white stone.
[3] *Lugens Sinus*, sc. Botany Bay.

Huc vestes et victus; agit secum omnia fossor.
Quadrijugos alii currus, alii esseda duro
Submittunt oneri, et meritos meliora caballos :
Inde viam faciunt.   Itur per rura, per urbes;
Quaque inculta capræ mordent juga; quaque
      cadentes
Lymphæ dulce sonant, et frondea procubat umbra.
   Nec tamen abruptæ cautes et fracta viarum
Offecere nihil. Sæpe acri in colle recusat
Taurus iter, nec voce potest nec verbere trudi.
Ergo alios addunt operi, gestuque minisque
Incendunt: hinc illa boum lamenta per agros,
Et gressus tenues, et noto longior ordo.
Multis auctumni pluviæ tristisque November
Obfuit: ut calido descendens imber ab Euro
Ad ver usque fremit, debacchatusque per arva
Stirpes et pecora et pavidos vi raptat agrestes.
Necnon æstivis in mensibus aridus aer
Ex Arcto venit, itque ferens morbosque sitimque :
Non umbræ frigus pecori, non tecta colono
Suffecere ; furit campis equa, deque profundis
Auditur sylvis vox intempesta luparum.
Hæc metuens, sub vere viam moliris, et acres

Sæpe memor recreas ad diversoria tauros.

Ni vocet hospitiis læti te cultor agelli,

Qui lac, et tostas fruges, et poma ministret

Dulcia : multus enim placidis in vallibus ævum

Degit adhuc, nec falcis amor, nec cessit aratri.

   Atque ubi longa diu circum deserta vaganti

Optati tandem incipient se prodere montes ;

Continuo saxis via crebrior, auraque tenuis

Signa dabit, clamorque virum, stridorque securis.

Mox immane vides agmen, tot moribus usos

Quot linguis armisque : riget coma, fronsque latro-

      num:

Instar habet ; sed mite genus, natumque labori.

Illi falce metunt, durisque ligonibus arvum ;

Cultro alius dirimit glebas, ac librat acerra ; [1]

Forsitan et puteos aliquis demisit in altum,

Statque inhians, si forte aurum, si forte recondant ;

Jamque solum digitis, jam forcipe preusat aheno.

Est quædam tabulis et cratibus apta supellex,

Quam cunas dixere : ferunt huc uberis arvi

Pondus, et injecta cogunt per vimina lympha.

---

[1] *Acerra.* sc. "an inspecting-pan."

Udæ eluctantur sordes ; quod restitit, aurum est ;
Signa palam dabit, ac digitis splendescet habendo.

    Talia molitos propior sol admonet undis,
Quicquid agunt proferre vetans in majus : at illi
Addunt ligna focis, stratique in littore duro
Accipiunt oculis et toto pectore noctem.

    Felix, qui tantos potuit perferre labores !
Quique procellarum furiis, æstuque, fameque
Majorem se fassus, iter patefecit habendi !
Fortunatus et ille, sui qui dives, et utens
Sorte data, magnis non invidet ! Improbus illum
Fors urget labor, arcta domus, rarique sodales :
At jucunda quies, at vivæ in montibus auræ,
Et vacuus curis animus, fecere beatum.
Patris amans illi soboles, nec læta laborum
Uxor abest : non ille timet de nocte latrones,
Non auctumnalem maturis frugibus imbrem.

CARMEN GRÆCUM.[1]

COMITIIS MAXIMIS RECITATUM.

A.D. M.DCCC.LV.

Ἔσσεται ἦμαρ ὅταν πότ᾽ ὀλώλῃ Ἴλιος ἰρή.

ΑΣΤΕΩΝ πόρθητορ, ἀτειρὲς Αἰών,
κρᾶθ᾽ ὅτῳ κισσὸς κυπαρίσσινοί τε
κλῶνες ἀμπέχουσι, μέλαν δ᾽ ὀπηδεῖ
    Δεῖμ᾽ ἀΐδης δέ,

ὀστέοις λαῶν ἐπιβὰς καμόντων·
ἔργα γὰρ θνατῶν τὸ παρ᾽ οὐδὲν ἡγεῖ·
παρθένων δ᾽ εἴ τις χάρις, εἴ τις ἀνδρῶν
    γίγνεται ἀλκά,

πάνθ᾽ ἅμ᾽ ἐξόλωλεν, ὅταν δοκῇ σοι,
λευκύπεπλ᾽ ὥσπερ ῥόδ᾽ ἐν ἦρος ὥρᾳ·
χα᾽ ᾽πιοῖσ᾽ αἰὲς γενεὰ τάφοις ἐν
    τᾶσδε χορεύει.

[1] University Prize Poem. Cambridge, 1855.

ἢ μέγ' ὀλβία πόλις, ἑστία τε
ἦν ποκ' εὔτεκνος Πριάμῳ· Σκαμάνδρῳ δ'
ἀμφὶ δίναις ἁδὺν ἔκλαγξεν ὕμνον,
    βωκόλος ἀνήρ,

πατρίδος γαίας τότε κῦδος αἰνῶν·
νῦν δέ, δύσδαιμον πόλις, οὔ σε λέξω
τῶν ἀπορθήτων· ἀπὸ γὰρ κέκαρσαι
    ὦ ποκ' ἔχαιρες

λάϊνον πύργων στεφάνωμα· κοὔ σοι
εἶδος, οὐδ' ἥβα, κορυθαίολ' Ἕκτορ,
ἤρκεσ' ἁ θάλλοισα τὸ μὴ οὐ δαμῆναι
    δουρὶ Πελασγῷ.

ὄλβιον δέ σ' εἶπον ὅμως, ὃς ἔγνως,
πρὶν μολεῖν, τἀπερχόμεν'· ὀλβία μοῖρ',
ὀλβία, πεπτωκέναι, οὐδ' ἰδεῖν πω
    δούλιον ἆμαρ,

ἄστυ θ' ἰμμένον πυρί, κἀν 'Αχαιαῖς
ναῦσι λευκὰς 'Ανδρομάχην παρειὰς
δάκρυσιν τέγγοισαν ἐπ' εὐρυκόλπῳ
    τήλοθι πόντῳ.

ἄλλος ὁ κρείων Βαβυλωνίας γᾶς
στᾶ ποκ' ἐν σεμνῷ θρόνῳ· εἵματ' ἐνδὺς
χρυσόπαστ', οἶνον δ' ἀπὸ δαιδάλω κρη
τῆρος ἀφύσσων·

εἶπε δ' οὐκ ἐπιστάμενος τὸ μέλλον·
" φέρτερος γάρ τις θεὸς εὔχεταί μου
φῦναι; οὐ πάντ' ἀμ' ἔσεται; " τὸ ῥηθὲν δ
οὐκ ἐτέλεσσεν.

ἦλθε γάρ, λέγοντος, ἄναυδος αὐδά,
χεὶρ ὁμοία μὲν βροτῷ, οὐ δ' ὁμοία·
οἱ δ' ἄρ' ἔφριξαν τρίχα, κἀλελίχθη
γούνατα τάρβει·

ἐκ δ' ἔφα μάντις θεῶ· " οὐ μάλα δήν,
οἷς πέποιθάς, σοι μενεῖ· ἀλλὰ κήδη
σὸν διῄρηται κράτος, ἆμαρ ἤδη
ὕστατον ἥκει."

ἦ· τὰ δ' οὐ χαμαὶ πέσεν· οὐκ ἄκραντον
οὐδὲν ὧν εἶπεν θεός· ἠφάνισται
ἀστέων ἄνασσα, κέκευθεν ὡς ναῦν
κῦμα θαλάσσας.

πάντα τοι μινυνθάδι᾽ ὅσσ᾽ ἔχει γᾶ·
κάππεσεν Ῥώμα ποκά, κάππεσεν δὲ
δαιμόνων μάτηρ ἰσοδαίμονός τε
       σπέρματος Ἑλλάς,

μυρίων Ἑλλὰς κιθαρῶν ἄγαλμα·
εἴπατ᾽, ὦ Νυμφᾶν χοροί, ἃς Ὑμήττω
λείμακες τέρψαν, πεφιλαμέν᾽ αἷς ἦν
       ἄντρα Λυκείω,

ποῖα δὴ δακρύσατε, τίς Κιθαιρὼν
ὕμμιν οὐ σύμφωνος, ἐπεὶ ναπαῖον
πρῶν᾽ ἰόστεπτον λίπετ᾽, ἄμβροτοι δ᾽ οὐκ
       ἔσσαν Ἀθᾶναι;

δόξα ποῦ κήνων ἄρα; ποῦ ποχ᾽ ὑμῶν,
νᾶσοι Αἰγαίας ἁλός; ἄφθιτον μὲν
ὕμμας ἀμπίσχει θέρος, ἁλίω δ᾽ οὔ
       πω φθινὰς αὐγά·

λοιπὰ δ᾽ ὅσσ᾽ ἄπαντα νέφος καλύπτει.
οὐκ ἐκεῖ χοροστασίαι καὶ ὕμνων
φθογγύς, οἷς Σαπφώ ποκα, χοῖς ἔχαιρεν
       Φοῖβος Ἀπόλλων·

ἠρέμ' αὖθ' ὁδοιπόρος ἐμβατεύει
ναμάτων ὄχθας, ὄπα δ' οὐκ ἀκούει
πλὴν στενοίσης ἀχόος ἀξένω δὲ
       τῆλε θαλάσσας.

ἵξεται δ', (ἴσμεν τόδε) κοὐχ ἑκὰς μάλ'
ἀμέρα, φθίνειν ὅτε καί σ' ἀνάγκα
'Αλβίων, αἱ νῦν ἀδιναί τε σωπά-
       σονται ἀγυιαί·

ἵξεται· τὸν μὲν χρόνον οὐκ ἐᾷ τιν'
ἱστορεῖν θνατῶν θεός· ἐν μέρει δ' ὧν
σὴ κατηφήσει χάρις, ὥστε μάτηρ
       τεκνολέτειρα,

αἴλινος δ' ἔσσει σποδός. ἴσμεν ὡς γᾶ
ἐστιν ἤδη γηραλέα· καὶ ὄρφνα
ὠρανῶ κρύψει πλάκα, χἄλιος δρό-
       μημα τελέσσει.

δεῖμ' ὅμως ταῦτ' οὐ φέρει ὃς καλῶς ζῇ·
τοῦτον οὐ τύμβου δνόφος, οὐ φοβάσει
ἐθνέων ἐρείπια, κἀκλιπόντες
       ἀστέρες οἴμους·

στὰς δ᾽ ἐπ᾽ ὠχραῖς ἀϊόνεσσι θάρσος
λήψεται, καίπερ μόνος, οὐ μονωθείς·
μνάμοσιν γάρ τοι φρεσὶν ἐγγεγράπται
    ῥῆμα παλαιὸν

οὐκ ἀμαυρῷ τέκτονος· "ἄλιος γὰρ
φέγγος οὐ δώσει· παρελεύσεται γᾶ
κὠρανὸς πρόπας· τὸ δ᾽ ἐμὸν μενεῖ ῥῆμ᾽
    ἄφθιτον αἰές."

*

LOCA SACRA APUD HIEROSOLYMAM.[1]

O FORTUNATI colles, domus ipsius olim
    Dicta Dei; si vester honos alia exsulat ora,
Nati si periere, jacentque in pulvere turres:
At solitos circa saltus dilectaque dudum
Saxa, morantur adhuc Solymæ queis gloria cordi:
Sæpe per anfractus nemorum exaudita querela
Virginis Hebrææ, dum trunco acclinis olivæ
Cantat bella patrum, residesque recalfacit ignes.
Quin[2] (si vera fides) sub amica vesperis hora
Mira manus tangit citharam, neque cernitur ulli:
Nec carmen terrestre sonat: sed qualiter undæ
Æquoris, aut, ventis ubi mota laborat, arundo.

    Nunc in densa rapi palmis juga, nunc in apricis

[1] University Prize Poem.   Cambridge, 1855.
[2] Conf. Heber's " Palestine : "
    " For oft 'tis said in Kedron's palmy vale
Mysterious harpings swell the midnight gale," &c.

Ire videmur agris, fontesque haurire sacratos:
Apparet quæ vallis aquam Cedronis 'opacat,
Et longæva micans inter querceta Siloe.
O ubi olivarum sedes, ubi clivus amatis
Accola relliquiis! video jam rura recludi
Bethaniæque casas procul, et qua pastor ab umbra.
Regnaturus iit populorum.   Hac illo fugavit
Valle feras; hæc antra loqui montesque docebat,
Dum labor unus oves, dum Pieris una voluptas.
Hinc persæpe Deus sera sub nocte redibat;
Hinc ingens, Solyma, exitium, ac venientia sero
Fata tibi cecinit: tuque aspernata canentem!

   Ergo inter cineres platearum ac diruta templa
Grassari permissum Italis: ergo occidit ingens
Gloria, et Isacidas matres sua forma reliquit.[1]
Tempore non alio spectatos sanguinis imbres
Dicunt, et simulacra rotis invecta coruscis,
Auditasque sonare tubas, inque aëre sudo
Fervere equum sonitus, atque arma minarier armis.
Agnovere quidem seri quid talia ferrent;

---

[1] Cf. Macc. i. 25, 26: " Therefore there was great mourning in Israel .... and the beauty of women was changed."

Tunc, quum summa dies aderat, templumque vora-
      bant

Vivi ignes :—quis Cyrus erit, qui fragmina rursus

Colligat, et patria extorres in sceptra reponat ?

   Ex illo furor Europes exhaustus in urbem

Atque Asiæ : tu, Nile, truces in proelia turmas

Misisti : quid signa crucis, quid ut orbis in arma

Hesperius ruerit dicam ?   Et nos fracta tuemur

Castella [1] in tumulis, famamque fovemus avorum.

   Nunc in colle sacro Turcæ dominantur, et intra

Ire nefas ; clausa avertit sese advena porta.

Devenit et tandem qua sola in valle quiescunt

Ossa sepultorum vatum.   Cape [2] missile saxum

Rite manu, ac tumulum nati exsecrator iniqui.

Ast ubi Gethsemanes lucos, ubi tristia calcas

Rura, et purpureos in opaco cespite flores,

Fama loci venit in mentem crimenque priorum.

His, credo, e latebris genitor natum egit ad aram

Chaldæus ; jam ligna manu, jam ceperat ignes ;

---

[1] Sc. some old castles built by Crusaders on the heights
near Bethany.

[2] Alluding to the custom of casting a stone at the tomb of
Absalom.

Ibat et hinc, torvo septus grege, sanctior illo
Victima, nec dubiam in cædem : perterrita tellus
Testis qui moreretur, et intempesta ruens nox,
Mota juga, et vivi passim per littora manes.

    Est locus [1] haud procul e muris, ubi cærulus aër,
Gleba ferax, et rubra vocant pomaria falcem :
Non uvis auctumnus eget, non ficubus æstas.
Huc olim (ut perhibent) nurus altæ stirpis origo
Venit inops : illis errabat collibus, illic
Sedit propter aquam, gremiumve replevit aristis.
Multaque præterea monstrat loca cognita famæ
Rusticus; uxoris [2] Syriæ sub rupe sepulcrum,
Et vatis deserta domum, quæque unda, quod antrum
Regis erant desiderium, regisque latebræ.
Dein loquitur—nec genua pudet flexisse loquen-
        tem—
His ut in hospitiis, hæc inter saxa, cubarit
Ipsa Dei soboles : quo tempore sidus Eoos
Præmonuit cœleste senes, volvique per auras

---

[1] Bethlehem.

[2] Uxoris—latebræ. Rachel's tomb, the wilderness of St.
John the Baptist, the well for which David longed, the cave
in which he cut off Saul's skirt.

Haud mortale melos pavidi sensere bubulci.

   Inde, reliquit ubi frondentem Taboris arcem

Sol, et Iordanis collucent stagna sub astris,

Vise silens thalamum[1] ingentem qua membra jace-

      bant

Illius, jam passa necem, jam debita coelo.

Cernis inauratas ut praeterlapsa columnas

Ingens turba virum incedat, longa oscula figens

Saepe solo, et lacrymis humectans grandibus aras?

Fracto alios saxo videas inhiare, sedili[2]

Quondam coelicolis; alii interiora morantur

Circum adyta, et rupem vel adhuc mirantur hian-

      tem,[3]

Signaque[4] marmorea nondum deleta sub ara.

   Tempus[5] erit (sic fama refert) quo nomine dicti

Illius, insuetas iterum per compita pompas

Ducent, inque novos solvet se terra triumphos

---

[1] Sc. the Holy Sepulchre.

[2] The stone where the two angels sat.

[3] The marks of the earthquake.

[4] The holes where the three crosses stood are still exhibited beneath the altar.

[5] Alluding to a Turkish tradition, that the Christians will one day enter the Golden Gate in triumph.

Ad sonitum Pæanis, et Aurea Porta patescet.

At, famæ male credentes, ad moenia [1] nota

Sæpe patres coëunt, et gentis quicquid ubique est

Judææ; regnumque orant, regemque morantem

Serius, atque umbra miseri oblectantur inani.

"Temnis adhuc proprios? O si, Exspectate, redires

His oculis, hac templa dares ætate renasci! "

    Scilicet et veniet, quem speravere tot anni,

Tot vatum cecinere lyræ: non ille puella

Natus matre, caput stabulis in agrestibus abdens:

Nocte latens aderit nimborum, alisque procellæ

Vectus; cum rutila stipabunt astra corona,

Atque in fronte geret non enarrabile nomen.

Ille novam ostendet Solymam, templa altera fessis

Gentibus; ipse dabit leges, ac sceptra tenebit;

Agnoscetque suos, atque agnoscetur ab illis.

[1] The Jews' place of mourning under the ruins of the temple wall.

I.   M

SONG.

" FAITHLESS SWALLOW."

FAITHLESS Swallow, fly away,
   To purer air and brighter day;
But when spring shall deck the plain,
   Swallow, come again !

Thou could'st not brook the changing sky,
Or Autumn winds that sadly sigh,
Too soon my fost'ring care forgot—
   And thou has left my cot.

When, thy weary wand'rings o'er,
Shelter thou shalt claim once more,
Smiles alone shall greet thee here,
   Swallow, do not fear !

IDEM LATINÈ REDDITUM.

CŒLUM ubi candidius te, perfida, defer, hirundo;
    Cœlum ubi candidius, splendidiorque dies:
Tempus erit tamen, arva redux quo pinget Aprilis;
    Illud ubi veniet, perfida, rursus ades.

Scilicet impatiens cœli mutabilis, et qui
    Triste sub auctumnum ventus anhelat, eras:
Hæc metuens, oblita manus quæ fovit egentem,
    A laribus nostris post breve tempus abis.

At cum fessa viæ, jam tandem erroribus actis,
    Hospitis officium, qualiter ante, petes,
Huc redeas ! reducem nos excipiemus, hirundo,
    Risibus assuetis; exue quemque metum,

Again I'll watch thy pinions light,
Around my head in airy flight,
Again thy faithless love forget,
    And give thee welcome yet!

Faithless Swallow, fly away,
To purer air and brighter day;
But when spring shall deck the plain,
    Swallow, come again!

Tecta levi rursus circumvectabere penna,
   Aeriumque oculis rite tuebor iter :
Utque prius spretos ultro obliviscar amores,
   Utque prius dicam, Sit tua nostra domus.

Ergo aliis infida locis te transfer hirundo,
   Lucet ubi cœlo candidiore dies :
At cum prata, novum jam ver induta, nitescent,
   Ne dubites nostrum rursus adire larem.

"JOHN ANDERSON, MY JO, JOHN."

John Anderson, my jo, John,
   When we were first acquent
Your locks were like the raven,
   Your bonnie brow was brent:
But now you're grawing auld, John,
   Your locks are like the snow;
Yet blessings on your frosty pow,
   John Anderson, my jo!

John Anderson, my jo, John,
   I wonder what ye mean,
To rise sae early in the morn,
   And sit sae late at e'en.
Ye'll blear out a' your e'e, John;
   And why should ye do so?
Gang sooner to your bed at e'en,
   John Anderson, my jo!

Ἀνδηρίδα, φίλ' ἀνδρῶν,
  τὰ πρῶτά μ' εἰσεφοίτας
τρίχ' ἐμφερὴς κορώνῃ
  καλὸν δὲ κρᾶτα λεῖος·
γέροντι νῦν ἔοικας,
  κάρα δὲ σὸν νιφαργές·
ὄναιο καὶ νιφαργοῦς,
  Ἀνδηρίδα, φίλ' ἀνδρῶν.

Ἀνδηρίδα, φίλ' ἀνδρῶν·
  τί δὴ μαθών, ἀναστὰς
ὑπ' ὄρθρον, εἶτα νυκτὸς
  ἐς ἀντόλας ἀγρυπνεῖς ;
φθερεῖς ἄρ' ὄσσε γ' ἄμφω·
  τίς ὧδε δρᾶν σ' ἀνάγκη ;
καθ' ὥραν ἕρπ' ἐς εὐνὴν,
  Ἀνδηρίδα, φίλ' ἀνδρῶν.

John Anderson, my jo, John,
    When Nature first began
To try her canny hand, John,
    Her masterwork was man.
And you amang them all, John,
    Sae trig frae top to toe,
She proved to be nae journeywork,
    John Anderson, my jo!

John Anderson, my jo, John,
    Ye were my first conceit;
And ye need na think it strange, John,
    Tho' I ca' ye trim and neat.
Though some folk say ye're auld, John,
    I ne'er can think ye so :
Ye're aye the same kin' mon to me,
    John Anderson, my jo !

John Anderson, my jo, John,
    We've seen our bairnies' bairns,
And yet, my ain John Anderson,
    I'm happy in your airms :

Ἀνδηρίδα, φίλ᾽ ἀνδρῶν·

   χειρουργίαν ποτ᾽ οὔπω

Ζεὺς ἐκμαθὼν ἀκμαῖον

   ἐκαίνισ᾽ ἔργον ἀνδράς·

σὲ δ᾽ ἐξέχοντα κἀνδρῶν

   σὲ πᾶν τὸ σῶμ᾽ ἀμεμφῆ,

οὐκ ἔκτισ᾽ ἐργατής τις

   Ἀνδηρίδα, φίλ᾽ ανδρῶν ;

Ἀνδηρίδα, φίλ᾽ ἀνδρῶν·

   νίος νέᾳ γὰρ ἅδες,

τί θαῦμα κἄν σε κομψὸν

   σὲ δ εὐπρεπῆ νομίζω ;

γέροντά σ᾽ εἶπον ἄλλοι·

   ἐμοὶ δε γ᾽ αἰὲν ἡβᾷς·

ὡς γὰρ πάλαι μ᾽ ἔτ᾽ εὖ δρᾷς,

   Ἀνδηρίδα, φίλ᾽ ἀνδρῶν.

Ἀνδηρίδα, φίλ᾽ ἀνδρῶν,

   τέκνων με τέκν᾽ ἰδοῦσαν

ἐν ἀγκάλαις ὑμῶς σαῖς

   μάλ᾽ ἀσμένην ἔθ᾽ αἱρεῖς·

And sae are ye in mine, John,
    I'm sure ye'll ne'er say no;
Though the days are gone that we hae seen,
    John Anderson, my jo!

John Anderson, my jo, John,
    We clamb the hill thegither,
And mony a canty day, John,
    We've had wi' ane anither:
Now we maun totter down, John;
    But hand in hand we'll go,
And sleep thegither at the foot,
    John Anderson, my jo!

                        BURNS.

μάλ' ἄσμενύς συ καυτύς·
  οὐ μὴ τόδ' ἀντιλέξεις·
κεὶ φροῦδ' ἃ δή ποτ' ἴσμεν,
  Ἀνδηρίδα, φίλ' ἀνδρῶν.

Ἀνδηρίδα, φίλ' ἀνδρῶν,
  συνεμποροῦντ' ἐς ἄκραν
εὐδαίμον' ἤματ' ἤδη
  πόλλ' ἔσχομεν συ κἀγώ.
πέδονδε χρὴ καθέρπειν,
  χεροῖν δ' ἔτ' ἐμπλακείσαιν·
ἐκεῖ δὲ συγκαθεύδειν,
  Ἀνδηρίδα, φίλ' ἀνδρῶν.

ON METRICAL TRANSLATION.[1]

(London Student, October 1868, p. 311.)

SIR,—A writer in a recent number[2] of this Magazine, laid down that there could be no true translation of a Greek or Roman poet which did not reproduce his metre; and that this had been successfully done by the Poet Laureate and others. I venture to think, on the contrary, that what resemblance there is between these modern experiments and their originals, is a *primâ facie* resemblance, and vanishes upon inspection; and that the specimens which the Laureate gave us, whatever may

[1] This and the two following articles afford a clear exposition of Calverley's views upon the subject of which he was so great a master, classical translation.—ED.

[2] The article here commented on will be found in the "London Student," for June, 1868, p. 149. (On Metrical Translation. By Henry Ward Fortescue.)—ED.

be their value upon other grounds, are, as imitations of metre, worthless.

That the likeness is not so perfect as it has been assumed to be may, perhaps, appear thus. Let us take Mr. Tennyson's alcaic stanzas—the best alcaics, one may well suppose, which our language is capable of producing—and consider a single line:

"Calm as a mariner out in ocean."

This, it will be said, is a perfectly unexceptionable English alcaic line. And such, no doubt, it is; but does it really reproduce Horace? If so, then, supposing we constructed a Latin line upon its model, we ought to have a *fac simile* of the normal Horatian line. Take

Sol ut in aëre lucet alto:

Is this a fair sample of Horace? It is a line which any elementary lyric-book would tell us was bad; a line the like of which could not be found in all Horace's Odes. The same experiment might be tried on any other metre with the same result. Coleridge's verse—

"In the pentameter aye falling in melody back,"

has been often quoted for its ingenuity and beauty, and I do not presume to question either.   I only say that a *fac simile* of it in Latin would be a pentameter so execrable, that the student of Ovid and Tibullus would hardly recognize it as a pentameter at all.

The truth I take to be this : that we modern experimentalists adopt—and I dare say must adopt, to make metrical composition possible at all in English—not merely a different, but a diametrically opposite, principle to what our predecessors followed.   We study to produce such verses as it shall be impossible to read without, at the same time, involuntarily scanning them.   They are to " scan themselves," to quote Dr. Whewell's phrase; or, as Mr. Fortescue puts it, " the words, read as they are spoken, should fall rightly into the metre." The ancients, I contend, made it a special point that their verses should *not* "scan themselves," and every form of line which did so they held bad on that account.   We select, in other words, for our standard precisely those lines which Horace or Ovid carefully excluded, frame verse after verse upon their model, and call the result a reproduction of Horace's or Ovid's versification.

My first proposition, as to the principle on which the moderns work, I need hardly verify. As to the second, it may of course be said, that we cannot tell how the Greek and Roman poets read their lines.

We have, however, this evidence as to how they did *not* read them. There are in every metre certain types of line which the writers in it manifestly avoided. In an alcaic ode (for instance) such a line as I propounded just now, or a line of the forms, " *Fortia corpora fudit Hector*," " *Fœda cadavera barbarorum*." A pentameter, again, ending with a monosyllable, would not be found in all Latin literature. And so with other metres. This avoidance is a simple fact, and one for which we are bound to account in some way.

Now if we suppose they meant their verses to be read as they are scanned, there is no apparent reason—I think I may say there is no conceivable reason—why any one of these types of line should have been objected to. " *Aùsa morì mulièr marìto*,"

and " Mòrdet aquà taciturnus àmnis" (read as
accented), are rhythmically identical with *fœda
cadavera barbarorum*, and with any other line which
scans.   A pentameter ending with a monosyllable
is rhythmically identical with any other pentameter
scanned : *e.g.*, there is surely no difference in sound
between " Sídera tángit equís," and " Sídera tán-
gite quís."   On that supposition, I say, all these
lines, which were as a matter of fact rejected,
would be perfectly admissible.   And in English,
where the supposition is true, they are all (as one
would expect) admitted freely.   I appeal to Mr.
Fortescue himself whether

> " Beautiful, innocent, unrepining—"
> " Crocus, anemone, tulip, iris—"

(which are identical in construction with two of my
model bad Latin lines)—would not be thought
rather good than otherwise in English.   As to any
objection to pentameters which end with a monosyllable, they do so almost uniformly.

If, on the other hand, we adopt the supposition
that the old poets (like the modern) read their
verses by an accent which was so far arbitrary that

it was wholly independent of the scansion, and was intended partially to conceal the scansion, then one sees at once why all these lines might have been disallowed. "Aúsa móri múlier maríto," and "Mórdet áqua tacitúrnus ámnis"—read as, rightly or wrongly, I was taught to read them at school— are two different lines, and are both good because they do not carry their scansion upon their face; and "Fortia corpora fudit Ajax" is bad because it does. This hypothesis, and no other that I can think of, would account for the condemnation of all the lines, in what metre soever, which are actually condemned. Why, for instance, would such a verse as

μελαῖνα νύξ, μελαῖνα νύξ, μελαῖνα νύξ,

be a bad iambic? The books would of course say that it has no cæsura. But why is a verse bad which has no cæsura? If all verses are to be scanned in reading them, a verse without a cæsura sounds just the same as a verse with any number.

What appears to me to be the almost universal fallacy of metrical writers is the assumption that when you have got the scansion of a line you have

I.   N

got its rhythm.   Mr. Fortescue speaks of "metre
or rhythm" throughout as convertible terms.   I
deny that the rhythm of the *Propria quæ maribus*
is the same as the rhythm of the "Æneid."   Any
metre may, no doubt, as he says, be imitated in
English : lines, that is, may be made in any metre
which scan.   Even so intricate a one as *Super alta
vectus Atys* is, I am told, copied, and that correctly,
in the Laureate's "Boadicea."

> "Adiitque opaca silvis redimita loca deæ."
> "Yell'd and shriek'd between her daughters o'er a
>   wild confederacy."
> "Soldier, sailor, tinker, tailor, gentleman, apothecary."

What the metre of the second and third may be,
and how far they correspond with the first, I am
not competent to say.   The last I had always mis-
taken for prose.   However, the lines in "Andro-
meda" are (most of them) undeniable hexameters :
but what then ?   The lines

> "When little Samuel woke and heard his Maker's voice,
> At every word He spoke, how much did he rejoice,"

are equally undeniable iambics : and the same
claim that Mr. Kingsley has to have reproduced

the rhythm of Homer, Dr. Watts has to have reproduced that of Æschylus.   I do not suppose that
if Mr. Fortescue had to translate the " Prometheus
Vinctus," he would feel obliged to represent the
iambic lines by the " Little Samuel" metre, and
the anapæstic ones by the metre of Owen Mere-
dith's " Lucile :" but I do not see how, consistently
with his principles, he could do otherwise.

Perhaps I may be allowed to make some com-
ments on Mr. Fortescue's own versions, to which
indeed he invites criticism——that is to say, on their
merits as imitations.   As to the first[1] ode, I should
say that he was bound, on his own showing, to translate it not only into sapphics but into Horatian sapphics.   It would be no imitation of Pope's metre,
for example, to write it as handled by Keats, or by
Mr. Morris.   Now the "dactyl in the middle," on
which Mr. Fortescue's sapphic line is made to
hinge, is *not*, I submit, a characteristic of Horace's
line.   It is there, of course, but it only appears

---

[1] The three odes, the translations of which are here criti-
cized, are Hor. Lib. i. Od. ii. Lib. i. Od. xxxiv. Lib. i.
Od. xiv.—ED.

when you take the verse to pieces: and I confess
that my despised old friend,

> " Sordid, unfeeling, reprobate, degraded "

seems to me more Horatian than any line in the
copy before me. Could Mr. Fortescue read the
ode he has translated into the metre into which he
has put it? Of course he could if he scanned it all
through ; and in that case I can only put my former
question in a different form. Why is it that we
never find in Horace such a line as

> *Ense nudo terruit Hector arcem ?—*

In an alcaic one naturally looks to the two final
lines. Of Mr. Fortescue's third lines, *one* seems to
me (for an obvious reason) really to resemble one
of Horace's : the remainder to be much less like it
than Mr. Jingle's fragment,

> " In hurry poste-haste for a licence."

They are all exactly in the metre

> " My brother Jack was nine in May,"

if we substitute a dissyllable ("April" suppose) for
the monosyllable at the end. Can Horace's third lines
be read, by scanning them or otherwise, into this

metre?   Some perhaps could, such as the first in
this ode; but that is no more a fair sample of
Horace's versification than

"Cornua velatarum obvertimus antennarum,"

is a fair sample of Virgil's.   Of the fourth lines, I
can only say that they scan too well; the scansion
is (of course intentionally) *pronounced* in all of
them: and consequently they are all precisely like
each other, and none, to my ear, at all like Horace.
As to the remaining ode, I should imagine that to a
person unacquainted with Horatian metres (and it
is for the benefit, I presume, of such that these
translations are made) the first two lines of every
stanza would appear to be lax Alexandrines, the
third the metre of " When the British warrior-
queen" (or of " Over rivers and mountains" occasionally, as in the case of the last stanza but two) ;
and the fourth no recognizable metre whatsoever.

One more criticism I would venture on upon a
different point.   I submit that " Trembled the "—
" Romans be "—" turn the helm" (though the next
word did not begin with a consonant)—are not

dactyls. Surely "helm" and "realm" are as distinctly long syllables as any can be. I do not mean to say that we are to conform rigorously to the Greek and Latin rules. I should admit that the second syllable of words like "disallowed," "warranted," or "organ-voiced" is short, and I think Mr. Tennyson made a false quantity when he placed "organ-voiced" where he did in the *Milton* alcaics. He might plead that without the aid of some actual Latin adjective such as "atlantean," or some exceptional English compound, such as "un-swan-like," for a central word, it seems impossible to imitate the most frequently recurring form of the Horatian third line. But at least we should remember that these rules were not arbitrary ones : it was from conformity to them, or rather to the theories of musical sound which they embodied, that the Greek verse derived its character, its melody and grace; and we cannot surely ignore them utterly, as most metrical writers habitually do, without sacrificing what really, much more than the metre, constitutes the essence and the "rhythm" of the verse. A Greek line is, in fact, a succession of vowels, separated by consonants introduced sparingly, and under such restrictions that it flows on uninterruptedly from syllable to syllable. The flow of an English line is generally choked (so to speak) by blocks of consonants thrown in *ad libitum*.

Compare

> " Silenced but unconvinced, when the story was ended,
>   the blacksmith,"

or,

> "Clasped each other's hand, and interchanged pledges
>   of friendship,"

with the first line of the "Iliad."   " Silenc'd but" is a dactyl, *encdb* a short syllable.   " Interchang'd pledges" is a reproduction of μῆνιν ἄειδε. Only conceive the havoc that we should make in one of Homer's lines if we inserted here and there such encumbrances as *ncdb*, *ngdpl*, or even Mr. Fortescue's *dth*, *nsb*, &c., between two of the short vowels. Compare again a pentameter by one of the very best of our metrical writers:—

> " Joyous knight-errant of God, thirsting for labour
>   and strife "—

with

"Impia quid dubitas Deianira mori."

The Latin pentameter of which the former is really a counterpart, is this :—

Troius ni terrent ob cor, versat per labor et stryx.

Does this bear the faintest resemblance to one of Ovid's pentameters?   I have a strong belief that any line which obeys the same laws of euphony as the Greeks and Romans observed—such a line as " The moan of doves in immemorial elms," or as many of Mr. Kingsley's own—resembles and reminds one of their poetry far more than these concatenations of so-called dactyls and spondees, which seem to me, even when they scan perfectly, to be not so much verses as skeletons of verses.

Metre (if I may end with a metaphor) is, in my view, a sort of framework whose office it is to support the verse.   It is possible to train a rose or a vine upon a trellis so that, while it adheres firmly, it is still left to follow its own devices and form its own pattern over the laths, which are only seen here and there amongst the leaves and tendrils.   It would also be possible to force every branch and spray into strict conformity with the lines of the frame, so that the outline of its squares should be the only outline visible.   The former method seems to me to be the way in which Homer and Virgil, and all poets ancient or modern, whose works I am linguist enough to read, have dealt with metre ; and the latter the way it is dealt with by metrical translators.

I am, Sir, yours very faithfully,

C. S. CALVERLEY.

THE " ÆNEID " OF VIRGIL.[1]

(Contributed to the " Pall Mall Gazette.")

A TRANSLATOR has two main duties to consider—his duty towards his original, and his
duty towards his readers. Translators of the old
school almost ignored the former consideration;
those of the new—amongst whom Professor Conington's " Horace," and in a less degree his " Æneid,"
justify us in classing him—on the contrary hold it
paramount. Specimens of translation on the older
principle may be found of course in Pope and
Dryden *passim :* in Lord Derby not unfrequently,
as when he renders

> " Dulces docta modos et citharæ sciens "—
> > "Skilled with transcendent art
> > To touch the lyre and breathe harmonious lays."

[1] " The Æneid of Virgil translated into English Verse."
By John Conington, M.A. (London : Longmans and Co.
1866.)

This is Horace done into Johnsonese : or rather
into that smooth commonplace which is nobody's
style in particular, and Horace's least of all.   Probably Brady and Tate went as far as it is possible
to go in this direction (though parallel instances
might be easily found in Pope) in transmuting the
single word " always " into

> " Through all the changing scenes of life,
>   In trouble and in joy."

We may take that as the extreme case of the one
school ; and Milton's " storms unwonted shall
admire," &c. (" procellas emirabitur insolens,"
κ. τ. λ.), as the extreme case of the other.

Professor Conington has not, as we hinted above,
dealt with Virgil quite as he dealt with Horace,
for reasons which he explains in his preface.   An
ode of Horace, he says, is for close scrutiny, an
Æneid for rapid reading.   Accordingly he has not
attempted to represent " the characteristic art of
Virgil's language."   He has not sought for equiva-
lents of his words or turns of speech—striving
rather to be readable, like Scott, than classical, like
Milton.

It may be said to this that Virgil's language *is* Virgil. His diction is an essential **part** of him; and Milton has taken such pains to show how it may be recast in English, that we cannot help wishing Professor Conington had elected to take more hints from him than he has **taken**; without becoming absolutely Miltonic, which would ill accord with Scott's metre. He has followed him at times, though perhaps unconsciously; wisely at any rate; as where—

"Night *invests* the world." (*Nox operit terras.*—Æn. iv. 352.)

cf. "Night invests the sea."—Par. Lost, i. 208.

At others he has not, when he might have done so with advantage; as in Æn. v. 113: "Et tuba commissos medio *canit* aggere ludos:"

> "And from a mound the trump *proclaims*
> The festal onset of the games."

This is good, but conventional compared with Milton's

> "To arms the matin trumpet *sang*."

Again, his

> "Wallowing, unwieldy, enormous—
> She knew not, eating death"—

are happy representations, one of a rhythm, and one of an idiom, so peculiar and characteristic as to be worth preserving. His " hope conceiving from despair " is palpably imitated from Virgil's

"Una salus victis, nullam sperare salutem,"

and expresses it perhaps more forcibly than Professor Conington's rendering, which is neat enough nevertheless.

But it is hardly fair to criticize Professor Conington for not having represented what he deliberately declines to represent. As a fair specimen of what he has done we will quote these lines (there are plenty as good) from Æn. vii. :—

> " With measured pace they march along
> And make their monarch's deeds their song;
> Like snow-white swans in liquid air,
> When homeward from their food they fare,
> And far and wide melodious notes
> Come rippling from their slender throats,
> While the broad stream and Asia's fen
> Reverberate to the sound again.
> Sure none had thought that countless crowd
>   A mail-clad company :
> It rather seemed a dusky cloud
> Of migrant fowl, that, hoarse and loud,
>   Press landward from the sea."

This passage from Book ii. seems to us very easy, and is most accurate :—

> " Meantime Heaven shifts from light to gloom,
>   And night ascends from Ocean's womb,
>   Involving in her shadow broad
>   Earth, sky, and Myrmidonian fraud :
>   And through the city, stretched at will,
>   Sleep the tired Trojans, and are still."

Here the third and fourth lines are absolutely literal. We will add one ingenious rendering of a line similar in character to the second, which latter, by the way, we thought bore a different meaning to that assigned to it :—[1]

> " Now *dews precipitate the night*,
>   And setting stars to rest invite."   (p. 35.)

These extracts will bear us out in saying that Professor Conington has produced a version singularly faithful (save in the point which he abandons), and pleasant and spirited withal, of a poem, as he remarks, little known to English readers.   He apologizes for appearing in the field after Dryden, and, we think, unnecessarily.   Dryden was a great

---

[1] [The line in question is in the original—" Vertitur interea cœlum, et ruit Oceano nox."—Æn. ii. 250.—Ed.]

poet, but not a translator at all. His "Virgil" is in no sense Virgil, but Dryden simply. We conceive, with all deference to Professor Conington, that there *was* a radical difference between the Roman and the "Caroline" poet; nay, more, that the heroic couplet (though opinions differ as to metres) is of its nature incapable of representing hexameters or any Latin measure except elegiacs, and perhaps Ovid's hexameters, which are elegiacs in disguise. We admit the professor's plea for the occasional use of "mote" (might), "eyne," &c., on the strength of Virgil's archaisms; though we protest against "treen," which appeared in one of "Horace's Odes," and which seemed to us not quite, but almost, as intolerable as "been" for the plural of "bee."

We may notice in conclusion one characteristic of Professor Conington's work which adds greatly to its value—that he never makes the vagueness of poetic phraseology a means of escape from a difficulty. A writer in "Fraser's Magazine" of September, upon recent translations of Horace (who ignores, by the way, Conington's "Horace" alto-

gether), gives us incidentally several model translations of his own, of which the following is a
sample :—

> " Me the poetic doves in days far-gone
>   Covered with fresh-cropt leaves, when found,
>   A truant child that dared to pass
>   Beyond my own Apulia's bound,
>   Sleeping in Vultur's mountain grass,
>   Tired out with lonely play in that long summer noon."

The last two lines, it will be observed, are represented in the Latin by " ludo fatigatumque somno ;"
except the one word " Vultur's." This we take to
be the worst translation possible ; not so much
because the text is absurdly spun out, and has a
perfectly gratuitous tail appended to it to eke
out a needless Alexandrine, as because " fatigatum
somno," the only ambiguous expression, is shirked
entirely. We would advise the writer, if he intends
completing the Odes, to glance meantime at Professor Conington's version of them, and if he is
preparing a criticism of recent translations of
Virgil, not to leave wholly unnoticed the very able
work we have just reviewed.

"HORÆ TENNYSONIANÆ."[1]

(Contributed to the " Pall Mall Gazette.")

TO those who still love occasionally to "brood and live again in memory with those old faces of their infancy" under whose supervision they acquired the art and mystery of Latin versification, and to try upon the *corpus vile poetarum hodiernorum* if their hand retains aught of its ancient cunning, the Laureate's works offer many attractions. Besides being, as Mr. Church proclaims him to be, "*poeta recentioris ætatis maximus,*" his muse is pre-eminently classical. He often consciously, often perhaps unconsciously, catches the tone of some ancient bard of Greece or of Rome.

---

[1] " Horae Tennysonianae ; sive Eclogae e Tennysono Latine Redditae." Cura A. J. Church, A.M. (London : Macmillan and Co. 1869.)

I.   O

He likes now and then to cull a phrase or a line
from one of them, and work it into his own poetry,
as—

    "This way and that dividing the swift mind."

Though he does not of course adopt the actual rules
of Latin prosody, his verse is framed always upon
the rhythmical principles of which those rules were
the embodiment; and in consequence there is the
same sort of grace and finish about it which distinguished the verse of Horace and of Virgil.
Between Horace especially, and the modern poet,
there exist, we think, in point of style and work-
manship, many similarities. A stanza of "In
Memoriam" is a thing compact, *teres atque rotun-
dum*, as is a stanza in a Horatian ode. Both
writers are equally intolerant of any but the right
word, and both have the gift of making it fit into
its place apparently by a happy accident. The
condensed phraseology, the abruptness, the ease
(attained probably "*per laborem plurimum*," until
art became a second nature) which characterize the
odes of Horace characterize also the cantos, so to
call them, of "In Memoriam." Even Mr. Tenny-

son's compound epithets are paralleled, and more
than paralleled, in Horace, and indeed in Virgil.
"*Zephyris agitata Tempe*" is as much a compound
epithet as "wind-swept" in English, and "*Segnes-
que nodum solvere Gratiæ*" is a three-barrelled compound epithet for which our language can furnish
no equivalent. Latin literature is, in fact, far
richer in elaborate compounds than English is, or
ever could be, since the Latin tongue expressed
naturally, by means of its inflections, what ours,
barren of inflections, can only indicate in an artificial way by inserting a hyphen ; *e.g.* that "wind"
is an ablative governed by "swept," a participle.
The contributors to the present volume, however,
have chosen to translate the Laureate, when he
writes any metre other than blank verse, into
Ovidian Elegiacs, rather than Horatian Alcaics or
Asclepiads. Two only, the Editor and Professor
Seeley, have constructed each an Alcaic Ode out of
the pages of "In Memoriam."

Of Mr. Church's Ode, which opens the volume (as
in its original English it opened Mr. Tennyson's),
we may speak in almost unqualified praise, and the

same may be said of his contributions generally. He has constantly succeeded in expressing most difficult English in Latin that is never forced and always forcible, as only a true scholar could. In only one case that we have noted he has made no attempt, and as we think wisely, to find an equivalent for the phrase before him :—

> " Nocturna luce coruscans
> Unda tuum molli geminabat murmure nomen,"

does not of course pretend to represent—

> " And rapt in wreaths of glowworm light
> The mellow breaker murmured Ida ; "

but to intimate that it cannot be represented. Should not "rapt" be "lapt," by the way ? Elsewhere "football" is printed for " footfall," and " spirited " for " spirted " purple. — How Mr. Church can deal with English which is not absolutely impossible, the following extracts may suffice to show :—

> " And doubtless unto thee is given
> A life that bears immortal fruit
> In such great offices as suit
> The full-grown energies of Heaven."

" Tu quoque jam peragis, credo, felicius ævum,
     Quodque facis nunquam mors abolebit opus ;
 Tu quoque, cælicolum jam viribus auctus adultis,
     Officio fungi nobiliore potes."

          " This garden-rose that I found,
          Forgetful of Maud and me,
          And lost in trouble and moving round
          Here at the head of a tinkling fall,
          And trying to pass to the sea."

 " Hanc equidem inveni oblitam dominæque meique,
     Hic ubi fit strepitus desilientis aquæ.
 Flos se perpetuos frustra volvebat in orbes,
     Si jungi æquoreis forte daretur aquis."

What can be prettier?   Mr. Church's version of
King Cophetua we think inferior to the preceding
one by Mr. Hessey, except the last stanza, which is
excellent.   *Per contra*, we prefer his rendering of
" As through the land at eve we went " to the
" altera versio " subjoined.

We have devoted some space to the editor and
largest contributor.   As we have mentioned Professor Seeley's Ode, we may add that we have no
possible fault to find, except with the first line, and
perhaps with the last, which latter probably could
not be put into Latin as simple as the English

within the space allotted. The first line *looks*, at
any rate, a terrific denunciation of the creature,
"the linnet born within the cage," which Mr.
Tennyson only says that he "envies not in any
mood." The accident of the first word being
printed in capitals gives to it a fictitious emphasis
and glare.—One of the editor's most able coad-
jutors is Mr. Kebbel, of Lincoln. *Notent tirones*
how "sandy bar" and "babble" are skilfully disposed of in the pentameter,

> "Visus arenosas increpuisse moras."

Tesquas reminds one unfortunately of Bland. No.
xxxiii. by the same author is a masterly production;
and take this extract from "Aylmer's Field:"—

> "The heads of chiefs and princes fall so fast,
> They cling together in the ghastly sack—
> The land all shambles."

> "Stricta ducum procerumque ruentia pulvere colla!
> Scilicet in tetris capiti caput hæret acervis.
> Cæde fluit tellus."

There are two good versions of "Come down, O
maid," by Messrs. Kebbel and Sotheby. The latter,
in an attempt on "Tears, idle tears," has, we should

say, like all his predecessors, signally failed. "Vivax" is not "fresh," nor

"Forma fenestrarum sensim quadratior exstat"

anything like

"The casement slowly grows a glimmering square."

The thing altogether is untranslatable. And the latter remark may possibly apply to

"Now sleeps the crimson petal, now the white," &c.

At any rate lines like these give, surely, no idea of the poetry and beauty of their original :—

"Regali in xysto cessat nutare cupressus,
Et niveus dormit purpureusque calyx;
Marmoreo nec pinna, vides? micat aurea labro:
Sed pyralis vigilat: tu mihi, cara, vaca!" &c.

These and all the succeeding verses appear to us worthless, till we come to the last four, which are graceful and good. Recurring to No. xxv., is *tamen* (on p. 83) used for "but"? We remember only one precedent, if so; Ovid's line—

"Nil mihi rescribas, attamen ipse veni,"

which has been variously emended. The true reading, which has lain hid from the interpreters, is, we have no doubt, "attagen," the *attagen Ionicus* of Horace, a bird whose name, dear to the epicure, would naturally pass into an equivalent for "deliciæ," as our English word "duck" is said to have done. The last syllable of *attagen* (vocative) would be, of course, short, *more Græco*.

Honourable mention ought to be made of Mr. Day, for a most able version of part of the "Lotus-eaters." The beginning of the poem is not done so successfully by another contributor:

> Eja! agite, o socii, validis incumbite remis;
> In manibus terræ—

is no translation whatever of the original; and the "wandering fields of barren foam" are wholly ignored, unless there is meant to be a glimpse of them in the final verse. Nor do we like "A Character" and "The Blackbird" as they appear here, from somewhat similar reasons, viz., that the Latin is vague and spun out. Lines 4-6 of the former are unintelligible without the English; and what the construction or the meaning is of the three last on the same page we have failed, even by the light of the English, to discover. The opening line does not scan at all, and the tenth from the end scans only by the skin of its teeth.

All this time we have omitted to notice what, considering the difficulty of the translator's task, and the ease with which it has been surmounted, is, perhaps, the gem of the volume—a set of Hendecasyllables, "O Swallow, Swallow," by the late Professor Conington. Every stanza is a feat of scholarship, and the whole makes a charming little poem. We quote one stanza—all are equally good :—

> " Procne nostra, volans volans ad Austrum,
> Lautis incide tectulis, ibique
> Quæ dico tibi dic meæ puellæ."

Of two or three other pieces by the same eminent hand we need only say that they are there.

Mr. Brodribb's " Tithonus " abounds in beautiful passages, which we would quote if we had space. Is not " kindly," however (p. 132), used in the sense of the " *kindly* fruits of the earth," and does not *genialis* mean something different? " Meus proprius," again, is, we think, only found in prose. Turning back to Mr. Church's poem on p. 17, *risu* seems to be used for *cum risu*, "smilingly." Is this legitimate? Surely you could not say, " Lacrymis sic fatur," unless "obortis" followed. " Risu cognoscere," " solvuntur risu," &c., are accountable enough. Then, is " Virgo inventrix " satisfactory for St. Cecily? does not *inventrix* want a genitive? We demur also to "male saucius," for "badly wounded," and are prepared to distinguish Horace's "male tussiit." Nor do we like " serrata " much more than we should "serrated" in the English. There are several words, such as *xystus, trichila*, and the prosaic *pedetentim*, which, it seems to us, unnecessarily mar this volume.

From the foregoing remarks it will be seen that we think highly of these translations as such. Whether or no it is pure waste of time to translate at all is a question upon which certainly much time has been wasted, and which, after all, concerns nobody except the translators. The title, we confess, puzzled us at first. The title-page hints that *Horæ* means here *Eclogæ Latinè redditæ*, which simplifies things; but then what is *Horæ Paulinæ?* Does "Tennysonian hours" mean hours during

which Tennyson was the presiding genius—hours
spent (by the contributors) in analyzing Tennyson ?
Anyhow these pages contain several admirable
specimens of an art believed by many to be doomed
—doomed, perhaps not even " after many a summer "—to decay and fall and pass away.

As in the heights of heaven the moon gleams
    clear, and around her
Shine in their beauty the stars, nor is one cloud
    moving in ether ;
Shines forth every cliff, and the jutting peaks of
    the headlands,
Forest and glen : then,—as opens the rifting fir-
    mament heavenwards,—
Star is revealed upon star : and gay is the heart of
    the herdsman :—
Not in less number than they, from the Xanthus'
    stream to the sea sands,
Glimmered the red watchfires that encompassed
    Ilion alway ;—
Glimmered amid Troy's host as a thousand stars ;
    and at each one

There sat threescore and ten, their face lighted up
    by the firebrand.
Meanwhile, each at his car, till crowned in her
    glory the morning
Roused them, their good steeds stood, white oats
    and barley before them.

SONNET.

WHEN o'er the world night spreads her mantle
    dun,
  In dreams, my love, I see those stars thine eyes
Lighting the dark; but when the royal sun
  Looks o'er the pines and fires the orient skies,
I bask no longer in thy beauty's ray,
  And lo! my world is bankrupt of delight:
Murk night seemed lately fair-complexioned day:
  Hope-bringing day seems now most doleful night.
End, weary day, that art no day to me!
  Return, fair night, to me the best of days!
But oh, my rose, whom in my dreams I see,
  Enkindle with like bliss my waking gaze!
Replete with thee, e'en hideous night grows fair,
Then what would sweet morn be, if thou wert there!

THE BOTTLING OF THE WASP.

THE wasps were one morning obtrusively gay :
    Said my true love, "I know what'll speed
        them away :
From a nail, or a chairback, a bottle hang down,
And they're ' tree'd '—the brave varmints that buzz
        round your crown ! "

He hath found an old bottle, I cannot say where ;
He hath bound it with skill to the back of a chair ;
Full of mild ale so yellow and sugar so brown ;
And he " tree'd " them by dozens, I bet you a
        crown.

They may talk of their hares, of their rabbits, and
        all,
Such round-headed rascals, in Westminster Hall.

But tell legislators, the things to put down
Are those queer little imps that encircle one's
    crown.

So here's to their health, when they next travel
    here :
The sugar's unrivalled, resistless the beer :
And in peace may they leave us, themselves while
    they drown
In the healthy malt liquor that's sold at the
    " Crown."

A LIFE IN THE COUNTRY.

(*Stanzas for Music.*)

" O H ! a life in the country how joyous,
　　How ineffably charming it is ;
With no ill-mannered crowds to annoy us,
　　Nor odious neighbours to quiz ! "
So murmured the beautiful Harriet
　　To the fondly affectionate Brown,
As they rolled in the flame-coloured chariot
　　From the nasty detestable town ;
Singing, "Oh, a life in the country how joyous,
How ineffably charming it is ! "

" I shall take a portfolio quite full
　　Of the sweetest conceivable glees ;
And at times manufacture delightful
　　Little odes to the doves in the trees.

I. P

There'll be dear little stockingless wretches
 In those hats that are so picturesque,
Who will make the deliciousest sketches,
 Which I'll place in my Theodore's desk ;
    And Oh, &c.

" Then how pleasant to study the habits
 Of the creatures we meet as we roam :
And perhaps keep a couple of rabbits,
 Or some fish and a bullfinch at home !
The larks, when the summer has brought 'em,
 Will sing overtures quite like Mozart's,
And the blackberries, dear, in the autumn,
 Will make the most exquisite tarts !
    And Oh, &c.

" The bells of the sheep will be ringing
 All day amid sweet-scented flowers,
As we sit by some rivulet singing
 About May and her beautiful bowers.
We'll take intellectual rambles
 In those balm-laden evenings of June,

And say it reminds one of Campbell's
  (Or somebody's) lines to the moon ;
              And Oh, &c.—it is."

But these charms began shortly to pall on
  The taste of the gay Mrs. Brown :
She hadn't a body to call on,
  Nor a soul that could make up a gown.
She was yearning to see her relations ;
  And besides had a troublesome cough ;
And in fact she was losing all patience,
  And exclaimed, " We must really be off,
Though a life in the country so joyous,
So ineffably charming it is."

"But this morning I noticed a beetle
  Crawl along on the dining-room floor.
If we stay till the summer, the heat 'll
  Infallibly bring out some more.
Now, few have a greater objection
  To beetles than Harriet Brown :
And, my dear, I think, on reflection—
  I should like to go back to the town.
             Though, &c."

APRIL:

OR, THE NEW HAT.[1]

[In deference to a prevalent taste this Poem is also a
Double Acrostic.]

Prologue.

MY Boots had been wash'd—well wash'd—in a
      show'r;
  But little I griev'd about that:
What I felt was the havock a single half-hour
  Had made with my costly new Hat.

For the Boot, tho' its lustre be dimm'd, shall as-
      sume
  Fresh sprightliness after a while.:
But what art may restore its original bloom,
  When once it hath flown, to the Tile?

------

[1] From " Punch."

I clomb to my perch, and the Horses (a bay
 And a brown) trotted off with a clatter:
The Driver look'd round in his affable way
 And said huskily " Who is your hatter ? "

I was pleas'd that he'd notic'd its shape and its
   shine,
 And as soon as we reached the *Old Druid*
I begg'd that he'd drink to my new Four-and-nine
 In a glass of his favourite Fluid.

A gratified smile sat, I own, on my lips
 When the Landlady called to the Master
(He was standing hard by with his hands on his
   hips)
 To " look at the gentleman's Castor ! "

I laugh'd, as an Organ-man paus'd in mid-air
 ('Twas an air that I happen'd to know
By a great foreign Maestro) expressly to stare
 At *ze gent wiz ze joli chapeau.*

Yet how swift is the transit from laughter to tears !
 Our glories, how fleeting are they !

That Hat might (with care) have adorn'd me for
    years;
  But 'twas ruin'd, alack, in a Day!

How I lov'd thee, my Bright One! I wrench in
    Remorse
  My hands from my Coat-tail and wring 'em:
" Why did not I, why, as a matter of course,
  When I purchas'd thee, purchase a Gingham ! "

THE CUCKOO.[1]

FORTH I wandered, years ago,
   When the summer sun was low,
And the forest all aglow
    With his light:
'Twas a day of cloudless skies;
When the trout neglects to rise,
And in vain the angler sighs
    For a bite.

And the cuckoo piped away—
How I love his simple lay,
O'er the cowslip fields of May
    As it floats!

[1] From " Scribner's Monthly."

May was over, and of course
He was just a little hoarse,
And appeared to me to force
      Certain notes.

Since Mid-April, men averred,
People's pulses, inly stirred
By the music of the bird,
      Had upleapt :
It was now the end of June ;
I reflected that he'd soon
Sing entirely out of tune,
      And I wept.

Looking up, I marked a maid
Float balloon-like o'er the glade,
Casting evermore a staid
      Glance around :
And I thrilled with sweet surprise
When she dropt, all virgin-wise,
First a courtesy, then her eyes,
      To the ground.

Other eyes have p'raps to you
Seemed ethereally blue,
But you see you never knew
  Kate Adair.
What a mien she had ! Her hat
With what dignity it sat
On the mystery, or mat,
  Of her hair !

We were neighbours. I had doff'd
Cap and hat to her so oft
That they both of them were soft
  In the brim :
I had gone out of my way
To bid e'en her sire good-day,
Though I wasn't, I may say,
  Fond of him :—

We had met, in streets and shops ;
But by rill or mazy copse,
Where your speech abruptly stops
  And you get

Dithyrambic ere you know it—.
Where, though nothing of a poet,
You intuitively go it—
              Never yet.

So my love had ne'er been told !
Till the day when out I strolled
And the jolly cuckoo trolled
              Forth his song,
Naught had passed between us two
Save a bashful ' How d'ye do '
And a blushing ' How do *you*
              Get along ? '

But that eve (how swift it passed !)
Words of fire flew from me fast
For the first time and the last
              In my life :
Low and lower drooped her chin,
As I murmured how I'd skin
Or behead myself to win
              Such a wife.

There we stood.   The squirrel leaped
Overhead : the throstle peeped
Through the leaves, all sunlight-steeped,
        Of the lime :
There we stood alone :—a third
Would have made the thing absurd :—
And she scarcely spoke a word
        All the time.

*   *   *   *

Katie junior (such a dear !)
Has attained her thirteenth year,
And declares she feels a queer
        Sort of shock—
Not unpleasant though at all—
When she hears a cuckoo call :
So I've purchased her a small
        Cuckoo-clock.

THE POET AND THE FLY.

(From " Aunt Judy's Magazine.")

PART I.

ROUND the Poet, ere he slumbered,
    Sang the Fly thro' hours unnumbered;
Sauntered, if he seemed to doze,
O'er the arch that was his nose,
Darting thence to re-appear
In his subtly-chambered ear:
When at last he slept right soundly,
It transfixed him so profoundly,
Caused him agony so horrid,
That he woke and smote his forehead
(It's the course that poets take
When they're trifled with) and spake:—

" Fly! Thy brisk unmeaning buzz
Would have roused the man of Uz;

And, besides thy buzzing, I
Fancy thou'rt a stinging fly.
Fly—who'rt peering, I am certain,
At me now from yonder curtain :
Busy, curious, thirsty fly
(As thou'rt clept, I well know why)—
Cease, if only for a single
Hour, to make my being tingle !
Flee to some loved haunt of thine ;
To the valleys where the kine,
Udder-deep in grasses cool,
Or the rushy-margined pool,
Strive to lash thy murmurous kin
(Vainly) from their dappled skin !
Round the steed's broad nostrils flit,
Till he foams and champs the bit,
And, reluctant to be bled,
Tosses high his lordly head.
I have seen a thing no larger
Than thyself assail a charger ;
He—who unconcerned would stand
All the braying of the band,
Who disdained trombone and drum—

Quailed before that little hum.
I have seen one flaunt his feelers
'Fore the steadiest of wheelers,
And at once the beast would bound,
Kangaroo-like, off the ground.
Lithe o'er moor and marish hie,
Like thy king, the Dragon-fly ;
With the burnished bee skim over
Sunlit uplands white with clover ;
Or, low-brooding on the lea,
Warn the swain of storms to be !
—Need I tell thee how to act ?
Do just anything in fact.
Haunt my cream ('twill make thee plump),
Filch my sugar, every lump ;
Round my matin-coat keep dodging,
In my necktie find a lodging
(Only, now that I reflect, I
Rather seldom wear a necktie);
Perforate my Sunday hat ;
(It's a new one—what of that ?)
Honeycomb my cheese, my favourite,
Thy researches will but flavour it ;

Spoil my dinner-beer, and sneak up
Basely to my evening tea-cup ;
Palter with my final toddy ;
But respect my face and body !
Hadst thou been a painted hornet,
Or a wasp, I might have borne it ;
But a common fly or gnat!
Come, my friend, get out of that."

Dancing down, the insect here
Stung him smartly on the ear ;
For a while—like some cheap earring—
Clung there, then retreated jeering.
(As men jeer, in prose or rhyme,
So may flies, in pantomime ;
We discern not in their buzz
Language, but the poet does.)

Long he deemed him at Death's door ;
Then sprang featly to the floor,
Seized his water-jug and drank its
Whole contents; hung several blankets
Round his lair and pinned them fast :

" I shall rest," he moaned, " at last."
But anon a ghastlier groan
To the shuddering night made known
That with blanket and with pin
He had shut the creature IN.

PART II.

WHILE unto dawn succeeded day,
Unresting still the Victim lay;
The many-limbed one had its way.

He heard the stair-clock's tranquil ticks;
When it exultingly struck six,
He gave a score or so of kicks.

" Before to-morrow's sun up-climbs,"
He feebly said, " yon leafy limes,
I'll write a letter to the ' Times.' "

Haggard and wan, when noon was nigh,
He rose and flung his window high;
He heard, beneath, an old man's cry.

He strove—but idly strove—to eat;
Till now, to see the potted meat
Vanish before him was a treat.

He strove to write, but strove in vain;
Dark thoughts 'gan shape them in his brain;
He listened to that old man's strain.

It rang out, maddeningly distinct;
As he gave ear to it he winked;
He dropped the pen that he had inked.

(Song of Old Man below.)

  "Catch-'em-alive!   Gentlemen, I've
Here such a dose as no fly can survive.
      House-fly, blue-bottle,
      Garden-fly—what'll
Save him when once he's got this in his throttle?
Let e'en a wasp dip his nose in the mixture,
Spread on a plate, and that wasp is a fixture.
      Buy, buy; give it a try;
Don't be put down by a poor little fly.

I.   Q

Who'll purchase any ?   Only a penny
Kills you them all, if it's ever so many."

He bought, he placed some on a plate ;
I wis, he had not long to wait ;
They ate it at a frightful rate.

But on his friend of yesternight
(He knew the animal by sight)
His baffled gaze could ne'er alight.

At last he noticed the unfeeling
Brute in a casual manner wheeling
Round an excrescence in the ceiling.

Self-poised, it eyed the heaps of slain ;
But, that it did not entertain
A thought of joining them, was plain.

It winged that upper-air till ten,
The bard's retiring-hour ; and then
Descending, tackled him again.

*   *   *   *

Next morn the young man made his will;
And either shot himself at drill
Or sucked slow poison through a quill.

The Thing accurst—the Vaticide—
All wiles for snaring him defied;
And at a good old age he died.

This tale (I guarantee it true),
Reader, I dedicate to you.
If you can find its moral, do.

TRANSLATIONS.[1]

I. FROM HEINE.

"So far from agreeable were his [Heine's] recollections of Hamburg, that when, in 1830, Mrs. Moscheles asked him to write in her album, he treated her to a satire on her native town, which we here give in the original, and an English version of the same."—*Life of Moscheles*, vol i. p. 195.

I CRAVE an ampler, worthier sphere :
    I'd liefer bleed at every vein
Than stifle 'mid these hucksters here,
    These lying slaves of paltry gain.

They eat, they drink; they're every whit
    As happy as their type, the mole ;
Large are their bounties—as the slit
    Through which they drop the poor man's dole.

[1] This and the two following translations were written for A. D. Coleridge's "Life of Moscheles" (itself an adaptation from the German).

With pipe in mouth they go their way,
   With hands in pockets; they are blest
With grand digestions: only *they*
   Are such hard morsels to digest!

The hand that's red with some dark deed,
   Some giant crime, were white as wool
Compared with these sleek saints, whose creed
   Is paying all their debts in full.

Ye clouds that sail to far-off lands,
   O waft me to what clime ye will;
To Lapland's snows, to Libya's sands,
   To the world's end—but onward still!

Take me, O clouds! They ne'er look down;
   But (proof of a discerning mind)
One moment hang o'er Hamburg town,
   The next they leave it leagues behind.

II. FROM J. F. CASTELLI.[1]

AT BEETHOVEN'S GRAVE.

FROM the high rock I marked a fountain breaking;
　　It poured its riches forth o'er glade and plain;
Where'er they streamed I saw new life awaking,
　　The grandam world was in her prime again;
To the charmed spot the tribes of earth came
　　　　thronging,
And stoopt to that pure wave with eager longing.

Yet of these hosts few only, keener-sighted
　　Than were their fellows, all its glamour knew :
The simple multitude surveyed, delighted
　　Its diamond glitter and its changing hue;
But—save unto those few that saw more clearly—
That wondrous fountain was a fountain merely.

[1] In "Life of Moscheles," vol. i. p. 167.

At last its source dried up, its torrent dwindled ;
 And all mankind discerned its virtue then ;
In minstrel's breast and bard's a fire was kindled,
 And brush and chisel vied with harp and pen :
But wild desire, and minstrelsy, and wailing,
To call it back to life were unavailing.

   *   *   *   *   *

Thou who sleep'st here, thy toil, thy bondage
  ended !
 Lo ! in that fountain's tale is told thine own.
Marvelled at oft, more oft misapprehended,
 By the few only thou wast truly known.
All shall exalt thee, now that low thou liest :
That thou may'st live, O deathless one, thou diest.

III. FROM J. F. CASTELLI.[1]

AT BEETHOVEN'S FUNERAL.

E V'RY tear that is shed by the mourner is holy ;
    When the dust of the mighty to earth is
        consigned,
When those he held dearest move sadly and slowly
    To the grave of the friend in whose heart they
        were shrined.

But our grief-stricken train is a wild sea that surges,
    That spreads to yon starry pavilion o'erhead
And girdles the globe : for all nature sings dirges,
    Where'er rings an echo, to-day o'er the dead.

But weep not for him : for yourselves sorrow only :
    Though proud was his place in the hierarchy
        here,

[1] In " Life of Moscheles," vol. i. p. 166.

This Earth might not hold him; his spirit was
    lonely,
  And yearned for a home in a loftier sphere.

So Heaven to the minstrel its portal uncloses;
  The Muse thither calls him, to sit by her side
And hear, from the throne where in bliss she reposes,
  His own hallow'd harmonies float far and wide.

Yet here, in our memories homed, he abideth;
    Round his name lives a glory that ne'er may grow
      dim;
Time fain would o'ertake him, but Time he derideth;
  The grisly Destroyer is distanced by him.

[Bey Ludwig van Beethoven's Leichenbegangniss (am. 29
           März, 1827).]

TRANSLATIONS OF HYMNS.

(FROM " THE HYMNARY." [1])

EASTER.

Concinet orbis cunctus, Alleluia. A Sequence. SARUM MISSAL.

ALLELUIA let the nations
    Sing to-day from West to East;
As they solemnize with praises
    And with prayers the Paschal feast.

And ye little ones be joyful,
    Whom the Holy Font hath made
White as snow: the lake that burneth
    Shall not make your ranks afraid.

---

[1] "The Hymnary; a Book of Church Song;" published by Novello, Ewer, and Co. To each hymn the number in "The Hymnary" is appended.

We, with you, to measured music
　　Fain would tune the slackened string ;
And in subtly-cadenced anthems
　　Bid our voices rise and ring.

Since for us, a mute meek Victim,
　　Christ endured the cross and shame :
He, the Living Life, a captive
　　Unto death for us became :

For our sakes He deigned to carry
　　To His lips the cup of gall :
Nail and spear, and pain and wounding,
　　In our cause He braved them all :

So through suffering He descended,
　　Laden with our sins, to hell ;
Whence He comes with many a trophy,
　　Telling that He triumphed well :

Death o'erthrown, He brake the weapons
　　Of His ancient foe in twain ;
And the third day lo ! He riseth,
　　In His flesh, to life again.

Sing we then to Him glad anthems,
  Who spread wide the heavenly door,
And to man gave life eternal:
  His be praise for evermore.   [271.]

EASTER.

Victimae paschali laudes immolent Christiani.   A Sequence of the 12th Century.

OUR salvation to obtain
   Christ our Passover is slain :
Unto Christ we Christians raise
This our sacrifice of praise.

By the Lamb the sheep were bought ;
By the Pure the guilty sought :
With their God were made at one
Sinners by the sinless Son.

In a dark mysterious strife
Closed the powers of Death and Life,
And the Lord of Life was slain :
Yet He liveth and doth reign.

" Say what saw'st thou, Mary, say,
As thou wentest on thy way."
" Christ's, the Living's, tomb ; the throes
Earth was torn with as He rose :

And the angels twain who bare
Witness that He was not there ;
And the grave-clothes of the Dead,
And the cloth that bound His head :

Christ our Hope is risen, and He
Goes before to Galilee."
Trust we Mary : she is true ;
Heed we not the faithless Jew.

Conqueror, King, to Thee we raise
This our sacrifice of praise :
We believe Thee risen indeed ;
Hear us, help us in our need.   [275.]

EASTER.

Panditur saxo tumulus remoto.   JEAN BAPTISTE SANTEUIL.
Paris Breviary.

THE stone is rolled away;
    The grave is bid display
Her secrets; through her charnel-chambers rings
    A voice; and lo, the dead
    Lifts his awakened head,
Lo, the deaf hearkens to the King of kings.

    O wondrous sight!   Again
    Life throbs in every vein:
Bound hand and foot and blindfold, on his way
    The dead goes forth alive;
    Doomed haply to survive
The multitude who mourn for him to-day.

  Thus Death himself, our foe,

  At last shall be laid low;

His chains rent piecemeal, and his slaves set free.

  That, which Thy Sovereign Power

  Hath wrought, O Christ, this hour

Is but an emblem of the things to be.

  Now to the Father, Son,

  And Spirit, ever One,

Be power ascribed by all things that have breath.

  In Thee, O Christ, we trust:

  When we return to dust,

Save us we pray Thee, from the second Death.

         [622.]

THE TRANSFIGURATION.

Quam nos potenter allicis.   JEAN BAPTISTE SANTEUIL.
Paris Breviary.

O CHRIST, how potent is Thy grace!
 Ne'er doth Thy loving-kindness fail,
Whether we see Thee through a veil,
 Or face to face.

Now His adopted sons are we
Who called Thee Son : our Surety thus
Gives His unfailing pledge to us
 Of bliss to be.

O Father, Son, what then was shewn,
Upon the Mount, the cloud dispelled ?
The types are gone ; the three beheld
 Truth stand alone.

I.   B

O feebly tracked by Faith's dim ray,
Lord, may we one day share Thy bliss;
See Thee; enjoy Thee; bursting this
    Our prison of clay.

To Him Who said, the bright cloud riven,
" This is My Son "; and, Son, to Thee;
To Thee, Blest Spirit; One in Three,
    All praise be given.   [368.]

THE TRANSFIGURATION.

Coelestis formam gloriae.   14th Century.

THE shadow of the glory which one day
    Christ's church on earth stands waiting to put
        on,
This morn did Christ upon the Mount display :
    There as the sun He shone.

That tale shall ages yet unborn record,
    How those three chosen gazed with awe-struck
        eye,
While Moses and Elias with the Lord
    Awhile held converse high.

The three great witnesses are gathered there
    Of Grace, Law, Prophecy : and, hark, aloud
To God the Son doth God the Father bear
    His witness from the cloud.

His Face aglow, His garments glistering white,
  So Christ foreshews what guerdon He prepares
For faith ; so tells them who in God delight
  What glory shall be theirs.

That mystery supreme, which they beheld
  Who saw the vision, lifts to heaven our gaze ;
And year by year, O Lord, our hearts are swelled
  With wonder and with praise.

O Father, from Thy sole-begotten Son
  And gracious Spirit separable ne'er ;
Dwell Thou within us, that, the battle won,
  Thy glory we may share.   [367.]

ASCENSION.

Felix dies mortalibus. JEAN BAPTISTE SANTEUIL.
Paris Breviary.

FOR aye shall mortals bless the day
   When with His Blood Christ won the way,
Incarnate God, to Heaven, and passed
Through its bright gates unbarred at last.

We are the members, He the Head :
We follow where our Prince hath led
And, one with Him on earth in love,
Shall share His throne in heaven above.

Gone hence, His own yet deem Him near,
For by His Spirit He is here :
As on the head depend the parts,
So rules one influence all our hearts.

But O that Day, that dreadful Day!
Whither shall sinners flee away
When, armed with vengeance, He shall come
Down from His throne to strike them dumb?

The just One, by the guilty called
Unjust, shall see them stand appalled,
Who once condemned Him, and resume
His Judgeship to pronounce their doom.

Man to redeem, whose due was death,
Christ freely yielded up His breath:
And, ah, what woe must they sustain
For whom His Blood was shed in vain!

Thou Who one day our Judge shalt be,
Jesu, all glory be to Thee:
All glory to the Father, Son,
And Holy Spirit, Three in One.   [317.]

ASCENSION.

Rector omnipotens die hodierno. HARTMANN,
a Monk of St. Gall.

LORD of all power and might,
 Mankind redeemèd, Who dost this day
  soar
Back to those realms of light
 Where Thou satt'st throned before :

Ere skyward Thou didst rise
Thou badst Apostles to the world proclaim
 God's pardon, and baptize
  All in the Triune Name.

Nor didst Thou let depart,
Lord, from the holy city Thine eleven,
 Till poured into their heart
  Was that last gift of heaven.

"Lo! but a few days hence
Ye shall no more be comfortless : I go
    To heaven, to send you thence
        One Who shall soothe your woe :

"And in Samaria ye,
And in Judæa and in Jerusalem,
    My witnesses shall be."
        So spake the Lord to them.

He spake : and as they gazed
A cloud received Him, marvellously bright ;
    With wistful eyes upraised
        They watched Him fade from sight :

Behold, two men stood near
Arrayed in white apparel ; and they said—
    "Why stand ye gazing here
        Into the heaven o'erhead ?

"This Jesus, to His Throne
Who this day riseth upon God's right hand,
    Shall come again, His own
        With usury to demand."

O God of earth, sea, sky;
Man, whom Thou madest, whom the Foe erewhile
From Eden forced to fly,
By craftiness and guile,

And dragged him to the night
Of death and darkness : and whom Thou, O Lord,
With Thine own Blood to light
And freedom hast restored :

Man yet again may win
The bliss he fell from : Thou hast paid the price ;
Thou bidd'st him enter in
Once more to Paradise.

Thou shalt return : and men
Hear from Thy lips their doom or their release.
Grant, we beseech Thee, then
To us eternal peace. [305.]

Sancti Spiritus adsit nobis gratia. KING ROBERT OF
FRANCE, OR ST. NOTKER.

COME, O Holy Ghost, within us ; and, removing
      by Thy grace
Every taint and tinge of evil, make our hearts Thy
      dwelling place.

Be with us, O quickening Spirit ; Thou canst pierce
      the deepest night :
Cleanse our base imaginations, change our dark-
      ness into light.

O Thou Holy One Who lovest wisdom always, be
      Thou kind,
By Thy mystical anointing heal the blindness of our
      mind.

Thou That purifiest all things, as none else beside
    Thee can,
Purify the clouded eyesight, Spirit, of our inner man;

That by us our Heavenly Father may at last be seen
    and known :
For the pure in heart shall see Him, and the pure
    in heart alone.

Fired by Thee the holy Prophets sang, of old,
    Messiah's birth;
By Thee fortified, Apostles bore Christ's banner
    o'er the earth.

When God spake, and as a fabric rose up earth and
    sea and sky,
Thou wast brooding on the waters, Blessed Spirit,
    fosteringly.

Still at Thy command the waters bring forth life, to
    quicken hearts;
Still Thy sacred inspiration unto man new life
    imparts.

Lord, Thou makest tongues of Babel one in worship
     and in speech :
Truth to them who bowed to idols, mighty Master,
     Thou dost teach.

Therefore when we kneel before Thee hear us,
     gracious Spirit, hear;
Prayers are all in vain without Thee, shall not reach
     the Father's ear.

Spirit, Who through all the ages hast instructed in
     Thy lore
Souls of saints that felt Thy presence like a shadow
     hovering o'er,

Dwelling now in Christ's Apostles, in a new and
     wondrous way,
And the gift of gifts bestowing, Thou hast glorified
     this day.   [322.]

WHITSUNTIDE.

Veni superne Spiritus.   CHARLES COFFIN.   Paris Breviary.

COME, O Spirit, from on high;
   Earth awaits Thee, parched and dry:
Dwell, O Lord, these souls within,
Which Christ's Blood hath cleansed from sin.

O redeem the pledge He gave
Ere the lustrous cloud He clave:
Dwell with us, no more to part,
And with fire baptize each heart.

For a Father lost we mourn;
Look upon us, left forlorn;
Heal our sorrows: only Thou
Canst give hope; O give it now.

Things that Christ in days of old
Did from simple babes withhold,
Things that they might hardly learn,
Let our riper minds discern.

Let the truths, which once a few
Priests and Prophets dimly knew,
Now be published by Thy grace
Freely among every race.

Let Thy holy influence draw
All men to Thee; let the Law,
Once on dumb stones graven, be
In our hearts writ legibly.

To the Father, glory be,
And the Son eternally,
And the Spirit, ever One
With the Father and the Son.   [320.]

WHITSUNTIDE.

Lux jucunda, lux insignis.   ADAM OF ST. VICTOR.

DAY all jubilant, all splendid,
　　When from heaven the Fire descended
　　　On the chosen of the Lord !
Heart is full, and tongue rejoices :
Yea, our hearts invite our voices
　　　To sing praise with one accord.

He Who ne'er His promise breaketh,
Thus His chosen Bride retaketh,
　　　On the Pentecostal day.
From the Rock, with honey teeming
Once, a gracious oil is streaming ;
　　　Never shall that Rock decay.

Writ on stone, not preached by flamèd
Tongues, the Law was once proclaimèd

From the mount in all men's view :
Hearts in Christ created newly,
Tongues in love united truly,
    Here are granted to a few.

O the joy, the exultation
Of that day when the foundation
    Of Christ's Holy Church was laid !
When she gave to God thanksgiving
For three thousand souls, her living
    Firstfruits, as they kneeled and prayed !

This the two wave-loaves portended
Of the Law :—two peoples, blended
    Into one—One God adore.
They were twain : until united
By the Stone the builders slighted,
    Never to be sundered more.

Not in vessels that are olden
Is the new wine meetly holden :
    Like Elisha, to the brim

All the widow's vessels filling,
Christ with sacred dew is willing
    To fill all who trust in Him.

Not to hearts by discord riven,
Shall these sacred gifts be given
    Precious dew, nor oil, nor wine:
Ne'er the Paraclete abideth
Within hearts which sin divideth,
    Shutting out the light divine.

Comforter, possess and cheer us !
Venom then shall not draw near us ;
    Hate shall flee before Thy face.
There is no delight, no sweetness,
Health, nor comfort, nor completeness,
    Where Thou dost withhold Thy grace.

Oil of gladness, Lamp uplifted,
Heavenly Bread, by Whom are gifted
    With strange power the springs and brooks;
New-create and pure, we render
Thus our thanks, on whom with tender
    Love, not hate, the Saviour looks.

I.   S

Gift, and Giver of all blessing,
Evermore be we addressing
    Praise, with lip and heart, to Thee !
Cleanse our sins ; in Christ renew us ;
And, when perfected, give to us
    Our eternal jubilee.   [324.]

WHITSUNTIDE.

Audimur: almo Spiritus. CHARLES COFFIN. Paris Breviary.

LO, the Father hears our prayer :
    Unto failing hearts to bear
All Christ promised ere He rose,
Forth to-day the Spirit goes.

As the Lord of Life draws nigh,
Signs and wonders multiply :
First through all the house there past
Sounds, as of a rushing blast ;

Flakes of fire fell fast, and hung,
Each one like a burning tongue,
In the pure thin air, and shed
Lustre upon every head.

Then the flames that lit each brow,
Passing thence—we know not how—
To their inmost spirit pour,
Light and strength unknown before.

Marvelling much the nations heard
Preached in every tongue the word;
All that seers had e'er discerned,
Told again in words that burned.

On the hearers then was poured
Forth the Spirit of the Lord:
Thick as sheaves at harvest-tide
They arose and prophesied.

Praise the Father, praise the Son:
Equal honour, too, be done
Unto Him, Who can inspire
Human hearts with flaming fire.   [321.]

THE VIGIL OF WHITSUNTIDE.

O Christe qui noster poli.   Paris Breviary.

O CHRIST, Who dost, our herald, rise
  Into the mansions of the skies :
Call, lift us, whom Thou here dost see
Prostrate and downcast, up to Thee.

Make us to haste with purest love
Unto the joys that are above,
Undreamed of by the earthly mind :
Faith can alone that treasure find.

There, the reward of labours past,
God gives His own Himself at last :
Their all in all is He, to bless
Their souls with perfect happiness.

Lord, from high heaven this holy tide
Send down Thy Spirit, Who shall guide
Us, by His all-prevailing grace,
To Thy most glorious dwelling-place.

Jesu, for ever glorified
Thou sittest by the Father's side;
All glory be to Father, Son,
And Spirit, while the ages run.   [318.]

WHITSUNTIDE.

Supreme Rector coelitum. Paris Breviary.

SOVEREIGN of Heaven, Who didst prevail
   O'er death, and with Thy life-blood dye
The path by which we hope to scale
    Yon starry sky :

Look down in mercy from Thy throne
   At God's right hand, O Lord, and see
Us who are lingering here alone,
    Orphaned of Thee.

Hear us, O Christ, for we were born
   Out of the travail of Thy soul ;
When by the spear Thy side was torn,
    To make us whole.

Thy toils and anguish at an end,
    Thou wearest now a glorious crown :
The hour is come ; send, Saviour, send
        Thy Spirit down.

O Jesu, glory be to Thee,
    To God's right hand Who didst ascend :
Glory to God, the One and Three
        World without end.   [319.]

TRINITY.

Benedicta sit beata Trinitas. A Sequence. SARUM MISSAL.

ALL blessing to the Blessed Three !
   Hail, co-eternal Deity,
In glory equal, Father, Son,
And Spirit; ever Three in One.

Ruling o'er all things, One in Will,
Three Persons, yet One Substance still:
The Uncreated Unity,
In Godhead One, in Persons Three.

This Faith can souls from sin release,
And bring them to that land of peace,
Where by the bright celestial throng
Is poured for aye triumphant song.

White-robed in Jesus' steps they tread,
Who sits enthroned above their head;
Their day of suffering past and gone,
Lo, they have put new raiment on.

Let us, in whom God's grace doth glow,
Pay now to God the debt we owe:
So, when to this world we have died,
Our place may still in heaven abide.

So, peradventure, when the last
Fight hath been fought and overpast,
We shall behold fair mansions rise,
To be our dwelling, in the skies;

' Where evermore a wondrous Light
Shines, inextinguishably bright:
It is the Vision of the blest,
The Lord Himself made manifest.

Its beams on angels' breasts it throws,
As on the Source from which it flows
They gaze,—the Form of Him Who trod
Erewhile this earth, Incarnate God.

On Him they gaze with burning thirst :
So shall the righteous burn, when first
They see the infinite reward
Assigned them by their Judge, the Lord.

[336.]

S. JOHN BAPTIST.

Praecursor altus luminis. VENERABLE BEDE.

HAIL harbinger of Morn :
Thou that art this day born,
And heraldest the Word with clarion voice!
Ye faithful ones, in him
Behold the dawning dim
Of the bright Day, and let your hearts rejoice.

John ;—by that chosen name
To call him, Gabriel came
By God's appointment from his home on high :
What deeds that babe should do
To manhood when he grew,
God sent His angel forth to testify.

Yet in his mother's womb,
To Him Who should illume

With light the nations John his witness bore :
        And when he came to birth,
        John first proclaimed to earth
That witness, and is glorious evermore.

        There hath none greater, none,
        Than Zachariah's son
Ris'n among those that are of woman born ;
        A prophet, he may claim
        More than a prophet's fame ;
Sublimer deeds than theirs his front adorn.

        Enough : can human speech
        Unto his glory reach,
Meetly may mortals herald forth his praise,
        For whom, in time of old,
        God bade His seer unfold
The mighty work ordained in after-days ?

        " Lo, to prepare Thy way,"
        Did God the Father say,
" Before Thy face My messenger I send,

Thy coming to forerun;

As on the orient sun

Doth the bright daystar morn by morn attend."

Praise therefore God most High;

Praise Him Who came to die

For us, His Son That liveth evermore;

And to the Spirit raise,

The Comforter, like praise,

While time endureth and when time is o'er.

[361.]

MARTYRS.

Supernae matris gaudia.   ADAM OF ST. VICTOR.

CHRIST'S Church in heaven to-day
   Rejoiceth : and rejoice, Christ's Church on earth.
We have our times of mourning and of mirth ;
   Their tears are wiped away.

   Succour Thy children, Lord,
Thy Church that in this joyless valley dwells :
Peopling the air, let angel sentinels
   Keep o'er her watch and ward.

   The world, the flesh, hell's powers
Wage differing war around us ; aye upstart
New phantom-hosts ; the sabbath of the heart,
   O Lord, it is not ours.

On earth we know no calm :
Fear succeeds Hope, Grief banishes Delight ;
In heaven they sing, and pause not day or night,
    Their never-ending psalm.

    O happy City ! Life
Is there but one long day of jubilee !
O happy citizens, for ever free
    From turmoil and from strife !

    They wax not old, nor faint :
They fear no treachery, flee before no foe ;
Gladness alone doth in each bosom glow ;
    One joy fills every saint.

    The blest one whom we sing
This day, now into Paradise received,
Beholds His Face in Whom he has believed ;
    He sees, unveiled, His King.

    May we too find a place
Among the habitations of the just,
This hour of anguish over; as our trust,
    O Lord, is in Thy grace.   [403.]

FESTIVALS OF APOSTLES.

Supreme, quales, Arbiter.   JEAN BAPTISTE SANTEUIL.
Paris Breviary.

O LORD, through instruments how weak
    Thou workest out Thy sovereign will !
Frail earthen vessels Thou dost seek,
    And with Thy choicest treasure fill.

And in due time the pitchers, charged
    With light, Thou dost in pieces dash;
And thence the light breaks forth, enlarged,
    As from the cloud the prisoned flash.

O'er earth Thy messengers are heard ;
    They haste like clouds before the gale ;
Fraught with the Word, the sacred Word,
    They pour forth thunder, lightning, hail.

I.   T

Christ is their war-cry : at its sound
 Are hell's proud citadels laid low :
So, while the trumpets clanged around,
 Fell once the walls of Jericho.

Lord, let these trumpet-blasts divine
 From treacherous sleep awake mankind ;
And let these lights, erst lit at Thine
 Disperse the darkness of our mind.

To Thee, on Thy Apostle's day,
 We pay all worship, God of might :
For thou hast callèd us that lay
 In darkness to Thy Glorious light. [389.]

BETHANY.

Intrante Christo Bethanicam domum.   Paris Breviary.

TO Bethany Christ comes, the leper's guest.
   Speed we then thither : Simon spreads for all
      The banquet : with the rest
         We flock to Simon's hall.

While Lazarus feasts, and Martha decks the board,
A box of odorous oil doth Mary take,
      Right costly ; to be poured
         Forth for her Master's sake.

She bathes His feet, and wipes them with her hair ;
She breaks the box, and all the oil is spilled
      Over His head : the air
         Seems with new fragrance filled.

O why do scornful hands at Mary point ?
Proud was her task ; this treasure did she save,
      Beforehand to anoint
         Christ's Body for the grave.

And, as His Faith is preached in every tongue,
And far-off lands to His allegiance won,
      Still shall o'er earth be sung
         This deed which she hath done.

Now to the Father and the Son uplift
High praise for ever ; Praise, and never cease,
      The Spirit ; through whose gift
         Christ's Bride hath perfect peace.

                      [625.]

DE DIE JUDICII.[1]

(Translated almost literally into the same metre as the original, with a rhyme added to make it an English metre, from an alphabetical hymn by Thomasius, published in Archbishop Trench's " Sacred Latin Poetry.")

CONCERNING THE DAY OF JUDGMENT.

A S a thief, who falls at midnight on his unsus-
           pecting prey,
  When we think not shall o'ertake us the Al-
           mighty's Judgment Day.
B rief shall seem to men the pleasures that they
           prized in times of yore,
  When they know that as a moment Time hath
           past, and is no more.

[1] This Translation is the last thing Calverley wrote for the press. It was finished a few weeks before his death, and was intended for " Good Words."—ED.

C langing over Earth's four quarters shall the sudden trumpet-call
    Summon unto Christ's tribunal, dead or living,
one and all :

D own from highest heaven descended, shining
angels hovering near,
    Shall the Judge in all the brightness of His
majesty appear.

E arth from pole to pole shall tremble, paling stars
shall shrink from sight ;
    And the sun himself be darkened, and the round
moon lose her light.

F ire shall execute, unbidden, his all-righteous
Lord's decree,
    Sky and lands in flame devouring, and the great
unfathomed sea.

G lorious shall the King be seated then upon His
throne on high,
    The attendant choirs of angels standing awed and
trembling by :

H is elect upon His right hand shall He bid their
station take ;
    While as goats of evil savour on His left the
wicked quake.

" I nto heavenly mansions enter," to the first shall
  say the Son,
 " Which My Father's love prepared you ere the
  ages had begun ;
K indly ye did once as brethren succour in His
  need your Lord ;
 Of your kindness of aforetime take ye now the
  rich reward."
" L ord," they shall exclaim, all joyous, " when
  beheld we Thee in need ?
 When to us didst thou for succour, thou the King
  most mighty, plead ?"
M ark the Judge Almighty's answer :—" When
  ye heard the poor man's plea ;
 Fed, clad, housed him ; lo, ye did it in your low-
  liness to Me."
N ext to those upon His left hand the All-Just their
  doom shall tell :
 " Hence ye cursed from My presence to the fiery
  flames of hell !
O nce I craved your ear a beggar, and ye reviled
  at My hard lot ;
 I was sick, and ye forsook Me ; naked, and ye
  clothed Me not."

P iteously shall ask the wicked : " Lord, when dealt
    we with Thee thus ?
  Sick or poor, when wast Thou mocked at, O most
    mighty King, by us ? "

Q uickly shall reply the High One : " When ye
    scorned the beggar's cry,
  Lo, the man whom ye thought scorn of in your
    wantonness was I."

R eeling back, shall then the wicked sink into the
    fiery glare,
  Where abides the worm that dies not, and the
    flames are quenchèd ne'er.

S atan with his servants lieth chained those dark-
    some depths beneath,
  Where for ever must the damnèd weep, and wail,
    and gnash the teeth.

T hen on wings shall mount the faithful, led by many
    an angel-band,
  To the realm of joy and gladness, to their hea-
    venly Father-land :

U pon them in perfect brilliance Light and Peace
    shall shine ; from them
  Veiled no more shall be that City, that supreme
    Jerusalem :

[1] **X** the King, in all the brightness of His
   Father's splendour decked,
  Face to face shall then be gazed on by the hosts
   of His elect.

Y e beware then of the Serpent and his wiles: up-
   hold the weak,
  Heed not gold, and flee vain pleasures, if the stars
   ye fain would seek:

Z one with Chastity's pure girdle day by day your
   loins, and turn,
  When the Master comes, to meet Him, bearing
   with you lamps that burn.

---

[1] There is an apparent hiatus in the alphabet of Thomasius here, U and V, like I and J, being treated as one letter. The claim, however, of V to be a distinct letter is so far recognized that it begins the next line in the couplet in the original as in the translation. There is no W in Latin, and no available X: so the author had to content himself with X^{tus}, and the translator has followed him.

www.ingramcontent.com/pod-product-compliance
Lightning Source LLC
Chambersburg PA
CBHW021040030726
47496CB00006B/1621